DISAPPEARING CITIES

DISAPPEARING CITIES

TONY FRY

ANTHEM PRESS

Anthem Press
An imprint of Wimbledon Publishing Company
www.anthempress.com

This edition first published in UK and USA 2026
by ANTHEM PRESS
75–76 Blackfriars Road, London SE1 8HA, UK
or PO Box 9779, London SW19 7ZG, UK
and
244 Madison Ave #116, New York, NY 10016, USA

© 2026 Tony Fry

British Library Cataloguing-in-Publication Data
A catalogue record for this book is available from the British Library.

Library of Congress Cataloging-in-Publication Data: 2025942479
A catalog record for this book has been requested.

ISBN-13: 978-1-83999-597-2 (Hbk) / 978-1-83999-598-9 (Pbk)
ISBN-10: 1-83999-597-1 (Hbk) / 1-83999-598-X (Pbk)

Cover Credit: Image created by Tony Fry

This title is also available as an eBook.

CONTENTS

ACKNOWLEDGEMENTS

This book would not have been possible without Italo Calvino's *Invisible Cities*. But in relation to it, as is said in Timor-Leste, it is 'same, same, different'. *Disappearing Cities*, it is not a product of imitation but one of inspiration. A special thanks goes to Anne-Marie Willis for editing, insight and more.

PROLOGUE

Fiction should not need qualification. It exists as it is – that is until there is an exception. Now a moment has arrived when fiction prefigures the real. If it can be imagined, it can be realised in time – that is until there is an exception. Italo Calvino is an exception. He writes about Venice in the form of fifty-five short stories that weave the city as a tapestry in a magical time of forms, signs, memory, desires, seen sights, names, the open and the sky, the hidden and the dead.[1] Here one is left with an impression of the city, and the imagined, as something made present by its absence, as with: a footprint, a memory, and above all, words – words of not just imagined cities that once were, or a city as perceived from historical imprinted impressions (the recall of childhood visits, and images from a story told, a book read, a movie seen). In this case, disappearance now travels ahead of appearance. Such is the character of the real as imagined.

• • •

'Bad news travels fast' – the phrase has been around since it was first coined by Thomas Kyd in his play *The Spanish Tragedy*, penned by him in the late sixteenth century.[2] Its truth applies sometimes, but not always. What now follows is an example of the latter; as such it is timely.

Reality/Fiction

We all live in a world where cities are disappearing. Mostly we don't see what's happening, but even if we are aware, the process appears to be very slow and with few examples. But historically it is not, and in geological time it is super-fast. No matter the present speed, the loss of cities is going to be huge. Unsurprisingly, the news of those already disappearing is not arriving, in large part because of where these cities are located; thus, the issue stays local. Moreover, cities, especially the old ones, look so real, established, solid and enduring. But the hand of disaster, the forces of nature and the bombs and missiles of war write a different story.

It is now evident that much of the future is inscribed in climate, biological and environmental data, climate change impacts, national security and economic risk analysis reports. Yet not many people, even if exposed to such material, can see the complete picture. The forces causing change to the present and shaping the future mostly go unseen, often with symptoms standing in for causes. Greenhouse gas emissions, toxic waste, the pollution of water, soil and air all have situated causal effects, but they are symptomatic of the conduct of industrialised societies and associated behaviours by organisations and individuals. Within such an industrial ecology, the larger the global population, the greater the demand for food, land, built fabric, employment, transportation, education, health care and more. Such demands never get fully met, and the more people, the greater the inequity. At the same time, the ways it is attempted to be met have proven to be unsustainable; hence the crises that now threaten the very continuity of life on Earth.

Here is the unwitting, or dismissed, environmental destruction that came from creating cities before, but especially after, industrialisation. Such action became inscribed in the knowledge and practices of design and making the elements and form of the city. This was carried out by numerous professions and trades that passed from one generation to another. As time passed, complexity layered upon complexity. The history of unsustainability is this under-recognised continual swing between knowledge and unknowing, making and unmaking that bonds creation to destruction.

The city is a harbinger of complexity and needs to be seen as such when asking: What destroys a city?

There are obvious answers, like war, fire, a volcanic eruption, an earthquake. The city is here one day and gone the next. But they are also destroyed slowly. A progression of heat is taking them toward unliveability, the slow creep of water levels of a rising sea or the gradual loss of freshwater. And then there is the devastation of a city's population by a pandemic, nuclear accident, a chemical spill; or the flight of a population from a city in rapid economic decline. Abandonment is followed by a descent into neglect and decay. All of these prospects, and more, are not only in play but are increasing, with enviro-climatic impacts and conflict at the top of the list. According to the Cambridge Centre for Risk Studies, of the top fifty cities at risk globally environmentally, eighteen are in S.E. Asia, nine are in China, nine are in the Middle East, six are in Latin America, and five are in North America.[3] These are major cities, such as Karachi (Pakistan), New Delhi (India), Manila (Philippines), Bangkok (Thailand), Lagos (Nigeria), Shenzhen (China), Ho Chi Minh City (Vietnam), Cairo (Egypt), Amsterdam (Netherlands), and Miami (USA). The fate of such cities is sealed. But the process of loss is not simple; it is usually gradual and complex. It should be added that the identification of risk does not mean it is acted upon. Lagos is a high-risk city, but it is also projected to be the largest city in the world by 2100, with a population of eighty million, the majority of whom are likely to be informally housed. In contrast, the top twenty of those cities least at risk (by being deemed as the most resilient) are all in the global North.[4] So said, the numbers produced by the kind of studies cited are always dated and indicative – the conditions of change are dynamic and accelerating. But what can be stated with certainty is that the risk levels are increasing.

It is also the case that responsive action is often contradictory: the Indonesian capital city of Jakarta is one example that makes this clear. As a result of its exposure to regular riverine flooding, coming sea level rises, and because it is sinking (due to groundwater extraction), along with high levels of pollution in the urban environment, the Indonesian government decided to abandon Jakarta. The nation's capital will be moved to a newly built one in Kalimantan (a region on the island of Borneo), which is part of the geographically distributed nation of Indonesia.[5] Fragments of Jakarta will have an afterlife, so traces will remain, but *the city that is* will have been lost. At the same time, building the new city means the destruction of a large area of native forest, substantial greenhouse gas emissions from construction works and significant negative impacts on the indigenous Dayak population of the region.

• • •

Now, to consider fiction. Not only does it often travel ahead of fact, but it can also constitute it. Imagination, as fiction's propellant, is frequently born out of seeing and projecting from observed actualities. It comes as a seeing otherwise, as a return from an imaginative mind meeting an object in the world or a worldly circumstance. So it is with cities: they beget cities, they are an accretion of imagination exercised, this in their overall form and in specific content. Viewed with imagination, and informed by empirical facts, there are circumstances where one can see the likely future and destiny of a city inscribed in its present.

• • •

None of the fictions that will follow are true; none of the cities named exist.[6] Yet truth is present and is evoked. It might well apply to your city, or a city near you, or maybe one that is a favoured holiday destination, or even a city you hold dear in a valued memory.

• • •

Our planet is just over four and a half billion years old. The first settlement, retrospectively, is deemed to be Çatalhöyük, built in southern Anatolia almost ten thousand years ago, for around ten thousand people. It can seem to some as if cities are eternal. Rome has even been called 'the eternal city'. But cosmically Rome, and all cities, are but a speck in time. Cities arrive, some flourish, others linger, a few prematurely die and then are forgotten; all are fated. Who remembers Çatalhöyük, Ur, Urak, Taxila or Shara Brae? No matter that almost the totality of the past is lost in time, it affirms the bad news that 'All that is solid melts into Air.'[7] Yet the assumption of, and desire for permanence pervades. Our sun will die, 'we' long before it: nothing is more certain than darkness.

• • •

The fictions to arrive here will be of fifty plus cities. Every one of them in some way disappears, and they portend the loss of a myriad of actual cities now destined to suffer similar fates. Disappearance does not just mean vanishing and so no longer existing. It also means moving from being visible to becoming a fading recollection, overlooked, unnoticed, inconsequential.

The forces of the destruction of cities are real; the names of the cities are not. However, in some cases, there are names behind the name. One now asks what stops the bad news that cities face from arriving. Besides the desire for permanence, there is something more prosaic (especially among politicians): dominantly, it is the fear of the flight of capital or people, a preoccupation with the exigencies of the present, and in some cases, the fear of panic. But then there is also something more fundamental – a failure to think in the medium of time, combined with a profound lack of imagination.

No matter who or where we are, no matter if we know it or not, we are living at a moment of epochal change. Our familiar worlds are fading away. What is unevenly arriving is a transformed, depleted and damaged one. The climate system has been destabilised, and the changes made to it are irreversible. Likewise, environments are being destroyed, and ecologies, species of plants and animals, are being lost. People around the world, especially the poorest, are increasingly being displaced as the land in which they live becomes uninhabitable as a result of heat, flood or fire. There are projections that displaced people could number in billions by the end of the century. Clearly, such change will take inequality to new extremes. Then there is the way technology changes us and our outer and inner lives at an ever-faster rate. At the same time, the power of technology corporations constantly grows. As they use their economic power politically, they have started to usurp the power of governments. There are now technology corporation billionaires whose wealth exceeds that of nations.

Against this backdrop, the majority of communities globally will, in their different circumstances, attempt to adapt to changing climate conditions as best they can in order to continue their existing way of life. Meanwhile, many of the planet's wealthy and privileged will increasingly withdraw into spaces of protection (from islands to geo-domes, bunkers and shelters, all artificially supported by technology – this process has already started.)

There is a clear danger that as the global enviro-climatic and security situation worsens, fatalism and nihilism will become the dominant psychology of most people everywhere. To counter these clearly perceptible trends, three absolutely critical actions need to be taken by individuals, organisations and government. This immediately rules out action by most people in nations in conflict, those that are dysfunctional and the vast majority of the socially resource-stretched nations of the 'global South', which is to say, the very countries most at risk!

First, the dangers have to be recognised and fully acknowledged without absolute proof of the certainty of every element of risk being realised. By the time everything is verified as certain, it would be too late to act.

Second, and linked to the first action, is the need for the dangers to be recognised. Simply presenting data, expert reports, media coverage of disasters and rhetorical statements by scientists and leaders of government organisations and NGOs does not deliver change. Unless one is already being impacted in some way, the immediate imperatives of everyday life and the appearance of a seemingly normal reality rule. This is for two reasons: one is *akrasia* (having knowledge but not letting it inform your actions), and the other is that to be 'modern' is to be chronophobic (chronophobia is the fear of time and the illusion of permanence).

Third, **pragmatically**, preventative actions need to be taken now, not later. This implies increased levels of action directed at mitigation, undertaking a great deal of contingency planning, and the commencement of large-scale projects for the adaptation of urban environments, food production and industry and commerce. All this action should already be underway; the fact that it is not is a mark of the failure of government from the local to the international across the planet. It links to actions one and two in *that if the scale of the dangers were recognised, imagined as experiential conditions, understood in time as escalating and negating our lives, and life in general,* **then** the political possibility of taking action that painfully restructures economic, social and domestic life **might** reluctantly be accepted by 'the people' and action taken by their leaders.

The stark truth is the gap between the advocation of *'adapt or die'* and its *realisation*. To grasp the danger that is real and palpable is to grasp the choice between **pragmatic** action or nothing. The block to recognising this cold, unwelcome fact of life is the mobilisation of reason to construct arguments and illusory actions of denial. The counteraction is not to employ substantialist reason against what would de facto be faux reason *but* to mobilise imagination to construct a verifiable, credible sense of the coming reality to deflect, avoid, mitigate. Here is the potential of the truth of fiction to overcome abstracted and avoided facts. We all know this, once we live and act in the knowledge that we are going to die. In order to live, we reach out and grasp life. This is what needs to happen collectively.

Fiction/Reality

But can fiction have transformative agency – can it create change, specifically, life-affirming action? The answer is an unequivocal yes. Put simply, the ability to imagine negative consequences and communicate them is constantly used to direct action. Imagining a possible disaster is used to inform preventative action. Fiction

designs. It is the means by which the imagination is materialised –
the philosopher Immanuel Kant bonded this to 'practical reason'.[8]
Fiction conspires with reality. It is more than a novel on a shelf.

The stories to be told are gathered around three themes. The first
theme is that the disappearance of cities is happening by natural
nature: in building cities on fault lines, on flood plains, in fire-
prone areas, below sea level, in cyclonic zones and by clearing land,
which creates environmentally damaged peri-urban environmental
conditions. Such action brings an increased risk of disease-carrying
animals coming into human contact (and with it the possibility of a
pandemic).

The next is the disappearance of cities due to unnatural nature:
what it names are actions by past and present generations, which
have changed the climate and set in motion its full array of related
impacts.

The final stories of the disappearance of cities are by purely
unnatural means, and they pertain to all those actions of direct
destruction, not least war.

DISAPPEARANCE
BY NATURAL NATURE ● 1

Natural forces have historically made cities disappear and have been doing so ever since cities first arrived. They will continue to do so. Volcanic eruptions, earthquakes, hurricanes, sandstorms, floods, tsunamis, landslides and plagues have all devastated major and minor cities. But the reason many of those cities were destroyed was that they were built in harm's way: on fault lines, near volcanoes, on flood plains and so on. As the global population has grown, as more cities have been built and as their populations have become much larger, so has the risk and likewise the impact of disasters increased. But now the situation has changed: the nature of nature has changed. It has done so as a result of our species' intended and unintended actions. Specifically, our intervention at scale in natural systems, for example, by emitting greenhouse gases (not least by combusting fossil fuels) that produce conditions that increase global warming, by land clearing, destroying forests and habitats, damming and polluting rivers and soil, dumping huge volumes of intractable non-biodegradable waste on land and at sea and in all reducing biodiversity. Not only do 'we' destroy the conditions we all depend upon, but in doing so, we equally do so for so many of our biological others.

The Moving Earth

ROMLEON

For many years, the City of Romleon, on the Island of D'Ore, had attracted visitors from around the world, in huge numbers. It became even more popular when, three years ago, it opened its Museum of the Future. It was designed by the renowned architect Lorenzo Chillo. The much-awarded building, along with its presentation of the future, was named by the International Association of Architects as one of the modern design wonders of the world. For this, Chillo was awarded its gold medal. The building's parabolic steel and glass structure was created to give the appearance of a giant teardrop falling to the earth. Architectural critics wrote about it profusely, with their articles appearing in scores of magazines and journals. Thereafter, the museum acquired the status of Chillo's masterwork.

The museum was built in the city on the site of a department store which several years ago had gone bankrupt. As the building was in poor condition, and as the demand for such stores in the age of online shopping was now non-existent, it was decided to demolish it and sell the land. This was duly done, and the City Council bought the site. The idea of Romleon having a new museum had been discussed for several years. They wanted one that was progressive and exciting rather than historical and conventional. A consultant was hired to explore options, and she proposed a museum of the future. The Council accepted the idea, and a concept design competition was launched, which of course Chillo won. It took eight months to design, two years to build and another year to install the museum's exhibits, which were created during its construction. All the exhibits were curated by globally renowned scientists, designers and artists, and all were funded by major institutes and foundations. The island, already famous for its beaches, food, casinos and flamenco music festival, with the addition of the museum, attracted even more people, especially culturally discerning tourists. It caused a boom in the already thriving hotel industry. Visiting the museum and staying at the museum's boutique hotel, also designed by Chillo, was on the bucket list of many of the world's young, rich, jet-set class.

The earthquake hit the island at 4.14 a.m. on a Sunday morning in early summer. The quake was 9.1 on the Richter scale. This magnitude made it one of the most powerful earthquakes for several decades. The most powerful in modern times was 9.5, in the Levant, and almost a century ago. Tragically, Romleon was the epicentre. Much of the museum was swallowed into fissures of the earth. Not a single building in the centre of the city was left standing. Over 17,500 people died, and twice as many were injured. More than 4,000 deaths were of hotel guests. Rescue teams arrived from different countries, and the body recovery process continued for three weeks. Only two people were found alive, both badly injured. Many bodies were impossible to recover. The nation was devastated by the event. A week of mourning was declared by the government. On a different scale of significance, so was Chillo and the world's architectural profession.

It did not require an expert in geology to pronounce rebuilding the city on the same site to be technically difficult and economically prohibitive. It was also the resting place of irretrievable bodies, two of whom were members of the City Council. The general view was that the site should be turned into a memorial park. Even doing this would be a major challenge. At this moment, rubble still marks the event of the disappearance of the city. The completely fenced site, which included the fated museum, had three high viewing platforms, at their feet piles of dead flowers. The crowds of visitors that once came to enjoy the city and the amazing museum are now replaced by mostly individuals and small groups who, usually in silence, view the ruin. Flowers from the gardens in a small park near the museum are starting to seed the site. It appears to be turning itself into a memorial park under its own volition.

YANOTI

Some lands were never meant to be lived on.

It felt like a truck had just smashed into the side of the house, but it was not. Big trucks don't travel down our road. There were cracks in the wall; they told me what had happened – an earthquake, but centred somewhere else. I turned the radio on, and there was just one repeating message:

'An earthquake and a Tsunami is progressing. If you are indoors, get under a strong table or desk. If outdoors, move into an empty space away from buildings. If you are driving, pull out of traffic, park and stay in the vehicle until the shaking ends. If you are near the ocean, quickly move to higher ground inland.'

I grabbed my keys, phone and bag. The kids were still in school. It was twelve past two, it was a twenty-minute walk away, but I could do it in fifteen.

All the children were away from the building in the far end school-yard in class groups. Each teacher was standing at the front talking to them. They were wearing high-vis vests with the class number on their backs. I grabbed my twins, Kiria and Tei. Parents were arriving, some hysterical, many covered in dust or dirt, and a few with evident minor injuries. Sirens of many different pitches were sounding from multiple directions. We knew the drill; we did it three times a year; things were under control.

The walk/run to the school had heightened my concern. The streets were full of people. There were more damaged buildings than I expected; some had collapsed, and many cars had smashed into walls or each other. I could see and smell smoke. There were emergency wardens in green helmets checking off the names of employees lined up outside office blocks. I cut across Tempi Park; the school was

on its west side. There was a police SUV, a van and several policemen and women standing around. One was standing on a bench
next to the van and speaking into a bullhorn: 'If you are a doctor
or a nurse, please report to the park police post immediately.' It was
clear that the centre of the city below us had been much harder hit.
Water could be seen; the tsunami had struck, but how badly could
not be seen. The waterfront was two kilometres from the city centre.
The National Bank tower, the tallest building in the city, was gone,
as were several other tall buildings.

Within fifteen minutes of my arrival, the yard became more
organised. My children and I, together with the parents who had
also arrived, were standing in line, one for each year, with their off-
spring. At the front, a teacher and a policewoman were sitting at a
desk. I was in the front third of my line, with Kiria and Tei beside
me, asking when we were going home. They were uncharacteristi-
cally quiet, as were many other children. When I got to the desk, I
saw the policewoman had a map with red and green areas marked.
I was asked for my address, which was in a green zone. I was told
that people living there would be allowed to return home once the
area was confirmed as being safe from aftershocks. Everyone in the
red zone had to go to an evacuation shelter not far from the school.
Going there was part of our emergency drill. All green zone people
were told to go to the park and await instruction from the police. A
food tent was being set up and blankets were being handed out. Not
a good sign. As we were leaving the school, I looked over towards a
group of maybe forty uncollected children. It was a sad sight; some
were crying. Teachers were trying to comfort them. I squeezed
Kiria's and Tei's hands. I was overwhelmed first with a sense of relief,
but then with sadness. I knew many of these children had lost one
or both parents that day. As I turned towards the park, there was an

aftershock tremor; it was mild but the reaction wasn't. There were screams and a few moments of chaos. Then there was an announcement from the police, who now had a PA system set up.

You will not return home today. There will be a meal provided at approximately six-thirty. Clean drinking water and paper cups will soon be available at four points in the park – please retain your cup. Blankets are now being distributed. Portable toilets are in the process of being delivered from the racecourse. The green zone is currently being inspected until dark, and inspections will resume at seven in the morning. More information will be provided as soon as it becomes available. We are sorry to inform you that the damage in the red zone is extensive and the numbers of the deceased and injured are high. The scale of damage and flooding means it will be some time before the actual scale of the disaster becomes clear. Please stay calm, make yourself as comfortable as you can and rest. No rain is expected. Our post will be staffed overnight. We will not disturb you again unless there is an emergency.

It was cool but not cold. We had three blankets. I put one of them on the ground and we would sleep under the other two. As we sat down, Kiria asked me a question that came out of his silence. 'Are we going to die?' I told him that we were not and 'that we had been lucky', but 'lots of people had not been and had died'. Immediately, Tei asked 'what makes earthquakes happen?' I tried to explain how there were huge slabs of rock under the ground that sometimes moved. When they did, everything above them started to shake. We talked about earthquakes for another five minutes or so, then Kiria bounced back with 'how do you know we aren't going to die?' My answer was that when we can feel the ground shaking, it is now very weak. The earthquake had almost run out of energy, and what was left would not kill us. He didn't look convinced. Tei wanted to know about dead bodies, 'Where are they?' and 'what happens when you die?' Answering safety at home is one thing; doing it in tragic circumstances is another. I realised that they would have classmates dealing directly with death. It was going to take them time to come to terms with what had happened, especially once they saw the scale of the damage and returned to a changed school community.

The children slept, but I kept waking. The ground was hard; there was another tremor around two in the morning. Breakfast was just tea and two very sweet biscuits. Just before nine we were told we could go home. We got back by nine-thirty. The cracks were worse than I had remembered. There was no power or water. We had food and would use what was in the now unfrozen fridge first. Getting candles and bottled water was going to be hard. There was at least a couple of weeks of life left in the radio batteries – the only radio we had. What was most certain was that uncertainty was going to rule for quite a while. Emotionally, the relief that the children were safe was huge; at the same time, I had never felt the pain of being a single parent with such intensity. All they had was me.

NASMIR

The city was built eighty metres plus above sea level along quarried coastal cliffs. The origin of the city was a village established in the early sixteenth century. Its last major addition was at the start of the nineteenth century. Since then, only just over one hundred houses have been built, most on sites of previous dwellings, although many old houses have been modernised. The gap between those houses and the cliff edge is only a few metres. Over recent decades, there have been significant tidal changes, an increase in average wind speeds, rising sea levels and more storms. As a result of these changes, coastal erosion has increased.

Rashid Rizq walked the path from his house to the top of the cliff, and back, every morning before breakfast. He had done this every day, no matter the weather, since he retired as the city's postmaster seventeen years ago. It now took him thirty-two minutes; when he first started, it took just twenty-five. On this particular day, he was about to leave his house when he noticed a fine crack in the wall to the right side of his front door. When he returned from his walk, he got a tape measure and measured its length, which was 'one point seven metres', running from just above the floor to the right at about sixty degrees. Within a week, it increased in length to 'one point eight metres'. It was no longer hairline but at least one millimetre wide. Rashid decided to phone the city engineer. He knew his late father well; they went to school together and were friends.

Within a week, an electronic measuring device was attached to the wall. Two weeks later, the cliff path was closed. Three cracks had appeared within an area of seventy metres. Now, two years later, the path has gone. Seven houses were condemned as being unsafe, including Rashid's, and all the residents were ordered to leave.

Rashid, in distress, moved in with his daughter's family. They had a small rural property five kilometres inland. His son-in-law was a police inspector in the city police force.

Three months after the move, Rashid had a visit from the city engineer, who told him the mayor was about to go public on a report from a geologist they had commissioned. It was very bad news. The erosion of the cliff would increase. Within twenty years, 15 per cent of the city would have to be evacuated; then, between eighty and one hundred years most of the city would be gone. Rashid was born in the city, as were his father and mother, and many generations before them. When he heard the news, he said nothing; he just cried. The last time he cried was when he learnt of his brother's death during the war over fifty years ago.

Wind-Force

DERON

Behind a vast expanse of banana plantations, to the front is the ocean. Deron is a banana port. Its roads are wide and dirt; its business buildings are two storeyed; and its houses are single-storeyed. Some are as old as the city itself, which is around one-hundred and seventy-four years. All buildings are timber-framed, with single-skin weatherboard cladding topped with an iron roof (the newer ones are actually Zincalume, but iron sounds better in rain.)

The city is in the 'Carra great wind belt' that each year brings a hurricane season that lasts several months. The city has no means of defence. It has never been totally destroyed but has been badly damaged. Its form reflects lessons learnt. The buildings are simple, cheap and, with the exception of the roofing framing, made from locally grown timber. When a building is destroyed, it is simply rebuilt within a few weeks, often with a good amount of timber salvaged from it. There is an acceptance of the fate of the place. The spirit of the city is one of pragmatic resignation to the way things are. Nobody is rich, except the ship owners and the people who own the plantations who occasionally pass through it. Likewise, nobody is poor. Everybody knows that one day a hurricane will come, there will be damage and a few people will likely die. But they also know that within a matter of weeks life will return to normal.

Somebody came from the government a year ago and told the elders that the ocean was rising and that in a hundred years the city would be flooded. Everyone knew it was rising. The fishermen had been telling people this for years, and anyway, a hundred years is a hundred years away. People pointed to a small hill along the coast, an hour's walk away, and laughed. Then they said to the government person, 'there will always be the hill, bananas, ships and our families.'

KORMARI

At a distance, it was black and created blackness. Up close, it was red and killed it.

Dust and sand arrived not just as a storm blocking out the sun but as a wind-powered force of destruction travelling at a hundred and forty kilometres an hour, leaving nothing untouched. The paint on metal is blasted off, the skin of an animal made raw and the bark of a tree stripped. Crops are torn from their roots and then buried. Then there is the sound, which is something like an all-enveloping low roar of a giant jet engine. Nothing else can be heard. It has no sense of ending; it hurts, it is a force of total erasure.

Kormari was a new small desert city, sixty-five kilometres from the capital. It had offices, apartment blocks and shopping malls. It had bars, cafes, restaurants, sports centres and gyms, a concert hall, a small conference centre, schools, a hospital and two parks, one with a swimming pool. It was an architectural template of a city created by people who made not a single concession to place.

Relentlessly, the dust and sand arrived over two days. It was not the first city to meet such an end. It would not be the last. It covered everything. In some places, it was a mere 30 metres high. In others, when backed up against large buildings, it rose even higher. It suffocated everything: systems, machines, daylight, people, animals. The city, in every respect, was buried alive. The event was unexpected, quick and final. The city had disappeared literally as a place and as part of the life of the nation. Who knows if it will ever be released from the claim of the desert? Beneath the dust and sand lay a quarter of a million people, the wealth of a dozen banks and countless unrealised futures. In the meantime, any 'solution' deferred, the perimeter was fenced and mined. 'Eyes in the sky' monitored it day and night – any identified detected incursion into the five hundred metre exclusion zone triggered a drone strike from the installed autonomous drone weapons system.

Cathora

Gordino saw the simple timber house he had been born in become matchwood. The first blast of wind took the roof off. Almost immediately, the walls were torn from the structure and thrown into the air, hanging there for a few moments before spearing into the ground at some distance and in different directions, shattering mostly on the rocks that lay between the house and the beach. The only thing that survived was the brick fireplace on which they cooked. He could not see his boat, nor the post to which it was moored.

Gordino and his wife Amira had watched the destruction from the slit window in the tiny stone cyclone shelter his grandfather had made when he built the house. It had been damaged before in other cyclones, but was always repairable. They did what they knew when news of a cyclone was broadcast – they took their wind-up radio, the tool box and enough food and water for two days to the shelter.

They had been married for three years and this was only the second time they had retreated to the shelter. They had been given the house when they married. Up until then, Gordino had lived in it with his father. Gordino's mother had died during childbirth. Upon giving his son and his wife the house, his father said that his working days were over and he was going to move into town and live with his brother. Juan, his father, had lost his leg just below the knee in a shark attack when Gordino was twelve. From then on, Juan mostly earned his living by making crayfish pots and nets. But he did teach his son how to fish, and by the age of fourteen his life as a fisher began.

As soon as the weather settled, Gordino started searching for what he could salvage from his destroyed house. At the end of the day, he had two piles of timber – a large one of firewood and a small one of mostly reusable floorboards and studding. Plus, a pile of roof iron; although dented, most of it was reusable; maybe six to eight new sheets would need to be bought. He also found wooden chairs that just had slight damage; their dining table had two broken legs that could be repaired. A box in which they kept linen was found undamaged. Bedding, lots of clothes, all wet and dirty, but washable, and kitchen items were found scattered around. There were no signs of his boots or their mattress. When he went looking in the rocks for his fishing nets, lines and baskets, he saw a lot of timber and parts of other buildings that had washed away. He and Amira dragged a section of a roof nearer to their shelter. The usable timber pile would now be bigger, and it looked like they would not have to buy roofing iron.

After a breakfast of bananas, bread and cold tea, they set out to walk to the town eight kilometres away. They would get there mid-morning. They passed two other wrecked houses – the first had been empty and abandoned; the second was lived in by a young family with a year-old baby and a three-year-old. Gordino and Amira checked out the house and the areas around it. There were no signs of life, or death. En route to the town, there was damage everywhere; many trees had been uprooted, some lying across the road. One had fallen on a car, but nobody was inside it. It was the same story when they got to the town, although there were many of the more substantial houses that had survived with damaged roofs and broken windows. Quite a few shops were wrecked. It looked like there had been some looting, with undamaged goods, mostly clothes, scattered around, clearly not by cyclonic winds.

When they got to Gordino's uncle Carlos's house, they found him and his father boarding up broken windows. Both were overjoyed to see them, although they knew they would be safe because of the shelter. Juan was especially upset to learn the house was gone.

An hour later they were sitting at the table eating chicken soup and talking about materials and rebuilding. Uncle Carlos would lend a tarp so they could make a temporary structure, some blankets as well as an old single-bed mattress they could double up on until they bought a new one after the house had been rebuilt. He would also lend Gordino a dinghy so he could continue to fish and afford to buy a new boat, which his father said he would give him a contribution toward. But nothing could get to the house site until the road was cleared, and this took five days. The next morning Gordino went to a hardware store nearby just before it opened and bought two large bags of 50 mm nails and two of 70 mm nails, plus a large bag of 60 mm galvanised roofing nails with washers. He knew in an hour or two they would have none. He then met up with Amira, who in the meantime had bought bread and vegetables. They both set off for home, with the tarp, rope and their purchases in a small handcart lent by his uncle. They would camp on the beach.

The next week was spent collecting more timber from the beach and sorting it for framing, studding, flooring and cladding, thereafter de-nailing it and then cutting it into standard lengths. Removing roof iron from the truss battens and sorting it was another substantial job. They also collected a lot of flyscreen netting. Windows would not be glazed but fitted with flyscreens and shutters. Gordino also found time to catch a few fish.

All off-cuts and smashed timber were tossed on the beach fire, along with other combustibles from collected waste, mostly timber, broken furniture, bedding and clothes. The fire burnt for a week. A whole lot of other things had also been washed up – toys, tyres, car seats, suitcases and more, which they collected into a large pile. There would be a huge amount of cleaning up to do. But there was a huge task of de-nailing the collected timber, cutting it to standard sizes, and Gordino and Amira were still doing this on day six when Juan and Carlos arrived with the mattress, bedding and boat, plus a large box of food and a collection of assorted crockery Juan had in a cupboard, along with more nails. Most of these things were leftovers from a vanished life. Like his brother, Carlos was a widower.

Within a week, Gordino, his dad and uncle had the frame of the house up. This time it was built with internal cross strapping to reinforce the walls. The roof also had joists more firmly pinned to the building frame – Gordino also had a net-ready cast over the roof that would be anchored to rocks he planned, with help, to roll into place. By the second week, they had applied weatherboard wall cladding, and by the end of week three, the roof was up. Thereafter, the floor was laid, and Juan was making and installing window shutters. The old smashed ones had been found, from which the hinges were removed and reused. By the Friday of week four, the house was finished, the mattress was on the floor, the table had four legs, there were the two found chairs, and a wooden bench Amira had found on the beach. The house was small, rough, solid and very basic. It needed more than one coat of paint; none was to be had, but it was a home. Carlos and Juan had arrived every day to help. At the end of the last day, he produced two bottles of red wine from behind the seat in his truck and celebrated the restoration of their fragment of the world. He also produced old bikes from the back of the truck, gifts to Gordino and Amira.

The day after the house was finished, the radio station came back on the air. Its mast had been damaged during the storm. The first item of news was that the City of Cathora, sixty-five kilometres up the coast, had been on the edge of the eye of the storm and had been wiped out with a large loss of life. That explained the huge amount of material on the beach. It also changed, in some way how Gordino felt about the situation. They partly benefited from the misfortune of others.

Within a few days, Gordino was fishing. As always, he caught enough for himself and Amira, plus an excess to take to sell to the fish stall in the town's market. He made a box and fitted it over the back wheel of his bike. Most weeks he sold a catch to the stall three or four times. Amira was also busy. She did something they both had talked about but never got around to doing – she created a vegetable garden. They were both trying to save to first buy a mattress, then a boat. It was going to take a while. They knew there would be more cyclones, but believed, and hoped, their simple house would survive.

RASKATT

As I remember it, the trek to the top of Somal took four hours. The volcano had been dormant for over three hundred years, but it was not dead. An occasional tiny puff of steam from the centre of the crater said so.

To enter the world of the creator's edge was to arrive in a cloud of mist and the gentle cacophony created by the chirps, whistles, chattering and buzzing of wings of a huge number of hummingbirds. The mist thinned, its opaqueness softened and the images of everything: small trees, plants, flowers and piercing colours of specular bromeliads appeared. It looks, feels and smells otherworldly. Environmentally, this is as exotic as it gets. The number and variety of colours of hummingbirds are astounding. It was the combination of all this that gave the whole vista a sense of unreal other-worldliness. I lost track of time, and it was dark when I got back to the base and my truck. The intensity of the experience, although sixteen years ago, has never left me.

I had arrived home a little late. I had stopped to drop two books off at the library and then went to the deli to get some cheese, bread and red seedless grapes. I arrived just in time to catch the 7 p.m. news. The first item was about the new director of the reserve bank. Not interested, but the second item grabbed me. Somal had erupted. There were dramatic pictures of it hurling rocks high into the sky and of lava spewing out of the crater flowing down the volcano's south side and heading for Raskatt a kilometre and a half away. The space between the volcano and the city was bisected by a river. I have no memory of what the rest of the content of the news was. I was lost in thoughts of panic in the city and the magic of life in the crater now extinguished.

They set my alarm so I would be up in time to watch the 5 a.m. news. Unsurprisingly, I had dreamt about my visit to Raskatt, where I had spent two days, and my hike up the volcano. The news was bad. The lava flow arrived at the river and pushed a massive wall of mud ahead of itself, and this mix of mud and lava flowed over the city. With the exception of the top of one church spire, the city was no longer visible, buried below many metres of this mass of material. Many people had fled, but it was estimated that 20,000 to 25,000 had been trapped and had died. Why did the people of the past build the city there? I knew the answer. The rich volcanic soil, the water from the river and the climate meant you could grow anything there. I remembered walking through the daily market at the centre of the city. Corn, potatoes, tomatoes, avocados, yams, chillies and numerous leaf vegetables, plus wonderful fruit: oranges, limes, mangoes, guavas, bananas, breadfruit, papaya – nature's abundance had sustained the local population for hundreds of years. It was their economy, the basis of their way of life and a major source of their nourishment. Yet its source, volcanic soil, remained.

While the city had disappeared, I knew the people who fled would be back. They would create more farms and gardens, and these would flourish for hundred years, or less, until Somal once again erupted. But the critical question will be, where to build the new city? Will it be in harm's way?

DONDROS

Cyclone Minura hit the coastal city of Dondros just after midnight. July was the start of the cyclone season. Warnings had been broadcast for the previous two days. Winds, travelling at over 160 kilometres per hour, were accompanied by heavy rain. By first light at 5:30 a.m., the extent of the damage was clear: the small coastal city had been wrecked; hardly a single building had not been badly damaged, many had been totally destroyed and flash flooding was serious. By the end of the day, emergency services announced that so far there were 541 fatalities and over 1,200 serious injuries. A disaster reception centre had been created at the Dondros golf club to the north of the city, where a medical triage and clearing centre had been established by mid-morning. During the day, there was a fleet of ambulances and three helicopters taking the injured to multiple hospitals around the country. Five evacuation centres had been created, four in the nearby city of Gallerier, which itself had suffered considerable damage, and the fifth at an army barracks of an infantry regiment not far from Gallerier. Coaches were bussing the 28,000-plus displaced adults and children to these centres all day.

A year later, the situation was still bad. Some people were still in Gallerier living in rented accommodation, caravan parks and temporary housing provided by the Council. Others had moved on to other parts of the country where they had family, friends or had found jobs. Some had bought and borrowed caravans and were living in them at the Dondros golf club – most of these people were small business owners. Many people were still waiting for, or arguing over, the settlement of insurance claims.

The state government had voted for the city to be rebuilt, not on the existing site but on higher ground three kilometres back from the sea. It stated it was not in a position to do this in the immediate future because of other costs created by the cyclone from impacts on infrastructure. However, relocation planning was underway. The land would be acquired by a mixture of land swaps and a small amount of land purchases. Land allocations to property owners would be indexed to the size and location of the prior property – the process would be slow and involve complex negotiations with displaced and existing landowners. The financial situation of owners who had totally lost property was even more complex, especially in relation to mortgages, business loans and the distribution of limited disaster relief funds and insurance claims. A lot of people had lost a lot of money. Many people had no income and had large debts they were unable to repay.

The material conditions were also complex. People were not allowed back into Dondros for several months. During this period, contractors were making the place safe, clearing roads covered in mud and the debris of smashed buildings. After this, the recovery of the stock of businesses, household goods and equipment by their owners began. Even when these people returned, there were major issues regarding their supervision and safety. A vast number of things were damaged during the cyclone and by the weather after the event over many months. Most of the machinery that survived needed to be cleaned and refurbished. Much of it had been under water or covered in mud. There were also issues with establishing ownership. Then there were fields full of wrecked cars piled high after being written off by insurance assessors, and mountains of building debris with household goods and furniture mixed in. It was a sad sight, but the sadness of wrecked lives was invisible. Lost lives, businesses, homes, belongings, expected futures – all gone in just a few hours of climatic violence, the experience cast into lifelong memory.

A container park was established in a field next to the golf club car park. Within it, listed recovered items and their recovery locations were stored. All lists were recorded in a register. There were also four large marquees full of equipment and machinery, including a wood chipper, several tractors, a crane and a water tanker. Everything on the register was open to be claimed for one year from the date of deposit. All unclaimed items would be auctioned. Most of the labour involved in this recovery process was voluntary. The other development was the material recovery programme. Materials from partly or seriously damaged buildings that could be reused were extracted and stockpiled – timber, steel (structural and roofing), doors and windows were the most common. Besides there being an economic argument for doing this, it was also symbolic. It represented a link and continuity between the old and the new. Another dimension to the action was an agreement with contractors on hiring labour from the displaced population. One of the key lessons of disaster is that psychological recovery has greatly helped people in some way to get physically engaged in dealing with the situation – it keeps helplessness at bay. It also plays a significant part in rebuilding the social infrastructure.

Dondros was just one disaster from Cyclone Minura. Seven other major settlements also received significant impacts. Over a quarter of a million people were displaced, over 6,000 people died and more than 14,500 people needed hospital care. This was beyond the capacity of the state to cope, and the federal government had to assist. The cyclone impacted three other states, although not as severely. All the indications from climate research and discernible patterns suggest that such events are going to occur more frequently. This prospect became a major media issue. Multiple sources ask: What action willthe government take in the face of this situation?

Disease

Dossop

Dr Singh has been a GP in the tropical city Dossop for five years. He was also a member of a research team in the Department of Tropical Medicine at the National University. He and the team, had been especially concerned with people increasingly presenting with a strange rash that started on their hands and arms and then spread to the rest of their bodies.

From blood samples taken from patients, pathologists in the department identify the condition to be a mutation of *Candida auris* – a yeast-based disease that has two strains – c and d. As an infection, it can develop in various parts of the body, especially in the ears, mouth, lungs and in open wounds. It can also spread to other parts without showing any detectable signs. Most young adults usually recover quickly, but this is not the case with children, for them it can be serious and terminal. The 'c' strain is airborne and can arrive and survive on material surfaces for several months. Within two months, two hundred and forty-seven small children and babies had died, as well as sixty-two elderly people. The city's population, especially the parents of young children, was in a state of panic. Thousands of these parents fled with their children, potentially spreading the disease elsewhere. Within three months, the population of the city, which had been 58,000 people here reduced to 37,000. Property values crashed, many businesses were in deep financial trouble as key workers had left and it was impossible to recruit new senior staff – a significant number closed. Again, the population shrank further.

No treatment for the condition was found. Mass spraying of surfaces on the streets, public transport, in shops and workplaces and in homes happened daily. The city smelt like a hospital treatment room. Fear gripped the city. Because the number of children living in the city became so small, the number of deaths dramatically fell. Schools barely functioned. However, older people continued to die, though not in large numbers. But the mood had been set. Ways of life changed. People stopped eating out, going to pubs and events of all kinds. People asked why there was a high level of fear and the claims of over-reaction. The answer was always the same: children.

The stigma the city developed went on growing. Nobody wanted to visit the place. It became a ghost town. Because of depopulation, the rates and taxes that the city Council depended upon all but dried up. Garbage stopped being collected, the streets stopped being cleaned, the parks stopped being cared for, public transport stopped running, the police and fire departments became depleted, supermarkets and many other businesses, including banks closed, doctors including Dr Sing left and the hospitals closed. The end came when the now emasculated Council terminated itself and informed the state and national government that the city had ceased to be operational. With their remaining funds, they created an 'assisted relocation fund' for people over sixty. Of the one-hundred and twenty of them still living in the city, fifty-five took advantage of it. Within a few months, there were just over two hundred people living in Dossop, with just one small corner grocery store still open. To get fuel, people had a two-hour return drive. Everyone lost money, lives were ruined and the source of the disease remained unknown but was deemed to be local. What happened made no sense.

KRISIC

It started almost unnoticed. People remarked that the summer seemed to be hotter and more humid than usual. The next year was a little worse, and again likewise the following year. Now the pattern was clear and everyone was worried.

The increased heat and humidity had two linked general and serious consequences for the health of members of the city's communities. The first was that people who perspired more became dehydrated and fatigued faster; they also experienced muscle cramps, Many of the older people also suffered from heat stroke, which increased their risk of heart attacks and strokes. The second was that increased humidity means vector-carried disease becomes more prevalent in the city as it was exposed to generally worsening conditions. This is because insects and animals that carry viruses, bacteria and parasites, like mosquitoes and rats, flourish in the climatic conditions experienced by the city. People are infected by being bitten or by eating food and drinking liquids that animals and insects have contaminated. The diseases that the vectors transmit include malaria, dengue fever, Chagas disease, yellow fever and parasitic diseases like trypanosomiasis (sleeping sickness) and schistosomiasis (a blood disease caused by parasitic worms). More recently, the risk of pandemics has increased as exposure to vector carriers has become more widespread and common.

The impact of humid conditions, besides affecting the population's health, also changes people's lifestyles – they spend more time indoors and, if they can afford it, in protected and air-conditioned environments. They also spend money on chemical-based insect protection and repellent products to protect their bodies in outdoor environments. By implication, people in the city who cannot afford such forms of protection have a higher rate of infection.

The people of Krisic, except for a small elite, were not wealthy. Like the majority of the nation, they were poor. Most of these people knew which insects and animals harmed them. However, they did not have medical knowledge based on an understanding of the consequences of increased levels of vector-borne diseases; instead, they did learn, by experience, the need to reduce their level of exposure to insects that attacked them. This meant that as things got worse; business for bars, cafés and music venues, all declined. People stopped attending sports events. They ceased gathering in public places and stayed home. The only businesses that did well were the take-away food outlets. Everyone knew that if the local economy collapsed, so would the city. One kind of fear collided with another.

Going outside was unpleasant. You had to cover yourself up to stop being bitten or stung. The smell of insecticide sprayed by the Council was always in the air. It seemed to make only a little difference, in part because it was not used in parks and gardens due to public resistance to the killing of pollinators, especially bees.

There was no cool breeze, just warm, moist air. People became depressed and short-tempered. They talked about the prospect of the situation just continuing to get worse. It felt like, within five or six years, the city would be unliveable. The death of the city was not going to be a sudden, traumatic event, but rather an unstoppable slow decline leading to its total abandonment.

Sky-Strikes

WENTERTON

It was a warm summer day, but cloudy. As usual, the public swimming pool was crowded. School was out. Lots of office workers were in the park eating their packed lunches. Every now and again, a car would drive past, windows down, blaring out the latest cool rap track at full volume from an overheated sound system, in some cases likely worth more than the car.

At 1:35, a few spots of rain were felt. By 1:40 it was heavy. At 1:42, small hailstones were pinging off car roofs. By 1:44 an invisible force cut in, and hailstones were the size of tennis balls. The noise was deafening. Windows and windscreens were being smashed, cars were colliding and suffering a great deal of body damage from the bombardment from above. People who were running for cover had fallen, some lying injured on the ice-covered ground. There were screams. Within a few more minutes, the sound of car alarms and ambulance and fire truck sirens added to the din. The event lasted maybe forty minutes, but it seemed like several hours. Reports from the outer suburbs and other towns and cities in the region indicated that their experience was, in some cases even more severe.

Media coverage stated that the hailstorm was the worst in recorded history. Four hundred people had died, and thousands injured. Hospital emergency rooms were unable to cope with the numbers arriving. The Fire and Rescue Service was dealing with fires caused by damaged electrical circuits shorting, fallen powerlines were arcing and people were trapped in vehicles. The ambulance service and the police were equally taken beyond their capability. Roofs were smashed, tens of thousands of vehicles were seriously damaged and vast numbers of trees had fallen on buildings, cars and roads. Trees left standing were badly disfigured, losing many branches; almost all lost their leaves. Roads were littered with debris everywhere, and ice covered every flat surface, contributing to the carnage on the roads: it took hours to thaw. Outside the city, crops of every kind were destroyed.

The federal government brought the army in to assist in the immediate task of clearing roads and covering damaged buildings that had lost their roofs. This would have included over half the buildings in the city. The task proved to be impossible: There were simply not enough people, tarpaulins, timber and rope available. It would take days to get more. Likewise, the demand for generators was huge and totally outstripped supply. Even though major contractors and the army supplied them, it was only possible to supply power to the most essential services, with hospitals at the top of the list. Hundreds of evacuation shelters were created in church halls and schools. Chaos and distress outstripped order for many hours.

It took a week to get the city functioning, three weeks to restore power and a year and a half to repair all the damage. It was not totally destroyed, but for several weeks, it felt so. For those weeks, everyday life was an engagement within a disaster zone. The legal, financial and insurance situation was very complex and had long-term implications for the city. For very many people, insurance was to become either unavailable or completely unaffordable. The cost of the clean-up, waste management, building repairs, the loss of business, loss of productivity, medical expenses, insurance payouts and costs for the uninsured were in the order of billions. The impact on mental health was also substantial. The public viewed the event as aberrant; the government knew otherwise but lacked a preventive strategy or a means to deal with the panic that may recur on a regular basis anywhere in the nation.

DISAPPEARANCE
BY UNNATURAL NATURE • 2

As a result of our species' intervention in natural systems –
anthropogenic climate change being a large and clear example
– many natural systems have ceased to function in previously
established patterns and cycles. Thus, the greenhouse gas emissions
from industrialised societies artificially created a transformation of
the climate with increasing levels of global warming, resulting in
a range of diverse environmental and ecological impacts. Natural
systems have been, and continue to be, changed by the consequences
of unnatural intervention. The changes produced are not discrete:
they relationally connect to other systems and conditions, often
producing serious and unwanted change.

The Rising Sea

SWURON

For many decades, the populations of the world's low-lying island nations knew that they were fated. The just over two and a half thousand people who lived on the island of Swuron confronted the prospect of the loss of their island home and decided to resist it.

The idea of how to resist came from Hubert Crowe, the owner of the biggest business on Swuron. Crowe Boatbuilding had built a few small ferries, in most years one or two coastal commercial fishing boats, and between six and ten wooden dinghies annually. The business was created by his grandfather, who handed it over to his two sons three years before he died, the elder being George, Hubert's father. He was the craftsman boatbuilder who taught Hubert his trade. Cedric, the younger of the brothers, was the businessman, storeman and the painter of boats. They employed three woodworkers, two machinists and two labourers. Hubert's father and uncle retired several years ago.

Swuron Council announced that it had received a report from the Government Department of Terrestrial and Marine Environments. It was a study of the island that the department had commissioned from the Institute of Marine Science at the National University. The report concluded that at the current rate of sea level rises, 19 per cent of the island would be inundated within twelve years – this including Swuron town. A special public meeting was held on the town's sports ground in mid-January. At this meeting, the report findings were announced; it was news that everyone already knew, this from leaky members of the Council. The CEO of the Council said that it had started looking at relocation options and that members of the public were welcome to present ideas and deposit them in a special mailbox that would be set up outside the Council office. Rather than do this, Hubert Crowe wrote a letter to the island's weekly newspaper, the *Swuron Herald*. It was printed on the front page and proposed a radical idea.

Crowe wrote that he had read a story in the *Shipping News* a year ago about an oil tanker, bought from a ship-breakers yard, that had been converted into a floating city. He said that he had done some research and found that the largest cruise liners accommodated up to 8,000 people, and the converted tanker half that number. He went on to say that the Council and the population should consider this kind of vessel as a possible solution that would allow us all to stay connected to the island. The idea was to multi-anchor the ship offshore and bridge it to the nearest land high point to the shore and intensively farm 26 per cent of the shrunken island. His research showed that rather than buy a tanker – which would have high cleaning costs – they should buy a decommissioned bulk carrier. One could be bought for between eight and ten million dollars, with towing and conversion costs to accommodate up to 3,000 people in comfortable, but modest-scale, apartments. To buy and convert would cost around twelve and a half million dollars, which equals just under five thousand dollars per person. The shipyard and other island material labour resources would be able to do the ship conversion. The ship would have a school, medical centre, sports facilities, shops, a laundry and cafes. The island would have farms and a small industrial and business complex. He said this does not add up to a utopia, but a quality of life can be created, and we can stay together. The letter invited people to drop a note into the Council mailbox just saying "interested". The mailbox overflowed. As a result, the Council decided to hold a ballot of everyone over fifteen years of age. The question was: If the ship conversion idea was established as viable, would you want to stay (tick box **A**) or relocate (tick box **B**).

The result of the ballot was 2,666 who wanted to stay and 441 who wanted to relocate – some of them really did want to leave, while others were just sceptical that the ship idea could be pulled off. The Council then approached the government, which did not dismiss the idea and agreed to fund a feasibility study. It was completed and was positive. The project went ahead in the form it was conceived and took two and a half years to realise, with the government providing 50 per cent of the funding. This was significantly less than the cost of relocation. In the end, two hundred and eighty-eight people opted to leave. They did so with a relocation grant from the Council, again matched by the government. One hundred and thirty-four of these people were under thirty, while the rest were between thirty and fifty.

The review of the development and business model of the project conducted during the feasibility study exposed a lack of skills in some areas. To deal with these issues, a range of positions was advertised on the mainland. This resulted in the appointment of 123 people, all between 25 and 42 – this significantly offset the leaver losses.

When completed, there were 320 people living in newly con-structed farm accommodation, which was very similar to the ship units. This workforce was made up of a poultry and livestock team, a cropping team, a horticulture team and a food processing team mill-ing wheat, rolling oats and making butter, cheese and yoghurt. A per-centage of the ship's population worked in the small industrial area where there was a weaving shed, a micro-brewery, a repair shop, a pottery and a machine shop supporting the enlarged boat yard, plus a grocery that also sold fish supplied by the two fisher families of the island whose boats had been built at Crowe's yard, and the island's school and small health clinic. All this, named the High Quay, was created on an area adjacent, and bridged to the ship, which was 10 metre above sea level. To the east, a large barn-like building had been constructed. While it had a café and functioned as a social centre, it was more than this. It was furnished with items donated from people's former homes; it was hung with signs and images from the abandoned town (stripped of all reusable material), and behind it relocated gravestones. Everyone called it the 'Big House'. While it was used for all kinds of social events and was the home of the sports club, above all it was a place of memory and stories. Then there were businesses on the ship: two cafes, a bar, hairdresser/barber, a laundry and a small sports club. There was also a telecoms and business hub that operated from the bridge of the ship. It provided a link to mainland services and ran the island's local area network.

Crowe shipbuilding yard was located 600 metres from the ship. Inspired by the ship conversion, it planned to buy, convert and sell smaller bulk carriers into 'floating communities' as an extension of its business. Its development was made possible by market interest gained from the profile the yard produced from media coverage of the island's ship, and later from the income generated by the project, plus an industry development loan from the government.

The island connection remained as it had always been: a weekly ferry that also brought supplies and mail. Overall, the sentiment that in different ways voiced how things have changed in the community came down to people saying things like, 'we've lost a lot, and gained a lot', 'it's been bittersweet', and 'we're glad to have a future, but we miss the life of the past'. The crunch will come with how many young people stay or leave (forever, or return). This in the large past will depend on how things are elsewhere.

GIURET

The settlement is on the Island of Polett, which is the largest of the ten in the archipelago. The town, which all who live there call a city, has a population of 1,072. People survive by fishing and farming. They say they have been doing this as long as stories have been told. The island has one shop that is open in the mornings four times each week. The people have very little money, but do not regard themselves as poor.

The island, which is 12.5 square kilometres, is getting smaller. Every year the sea takes back two metres of shoreline. It has been clear for several years that the 'city' will have to move. It is very close to the sea, and over the last decade it has lost seventeen houses to coastal erosion. The Council has been talking to the government and requesting financial support to assist with relocating. The plan is to buy small prefabricated houses with a living room, two bedrooms, a bathroom and a kitchen with a veranda. Up until now the sea has been the bathroom, it will remain so for many people. The new bathroom will have a shower, a hand basin and an attached composting toilet. Water will come from a roof-mounted tank refilled by a solar pump drawing from the to-be-created island reticulated water supply from its bore. They also asked the government to provide the island with a new small tractor and to send a contractor with a bulldozer to clear higher elevation land for farm resettlement.

Not all the islands in the archipelago will survive. Four are only just over a metre above sea level. The expectation is that the population of Polett will grow by about 200 in the coming years as displaced people arrive. The government does not expect the island to have a long-term future. Based on current projected sea rise data, the island will lose 40 per cent of its land mass in the next century and a half.

There is an ongoing argument in government that the proposed relocation is just a stop-gap action and is a misuse of funds, and would be more socially and economically responsible to undertake a major relocation to the mainland. The argument continues, but this position is likely to prevail.

Cavarone

The tropical delta city of Cavarone, with its beautiful beaches, fine eating houses, opulent casinos, wild nightclubs, famed theatre cafes and excellent bars, was one of the most celebrated playgrounds of the rich in the world. Its downfall was its proximity to the ocean and the fact that the city was built on a flood plain, which nobody expected would ever flood. That illusion had a life many decades ago, but now a new reality has arrived and perceptions have changed; this storm surge destroyed buildings. The seriousness of climate change–induced sea level rises has become recognised. It was therefore no great surprise, but disturbing, when the City Council announced that the city was at risk and would need to relocate within five years. This announcement arrived without any transition plan, consultation or sense of contingency. As a result, capital quickly started to ebb away. Nightclubs and bars were the first businesses to close. Within eighteen months, 'the strip' was dead, banks had closed and visitor numbers had plummeted. As the businesses closed, the many young singles they employed moved on. Families also left, but not as many or as quickly.

Rolando De Santo, one of the new generation of 'multi-dimensional entrepreneurs' who diversified by 'platforming' upon initial property developments. Rather than just 'fitting out' a building he 'fitted out' a whole block-sized project – this with its own water, waste management, power system, communication infrastructure, entertainment infrastructure and image. His company Autonomous Systemic Developments (ASD) was based on a principle of maximising community capital extraction. He built the homes and workplaces, created the businesses that employed the local population and owned the businesses where they spent their income. This was not a new idea.

For example, in the late 1880s, an owner of a 'railroad luxury car company', in what was to become the most powerful nation in the world, created a workforce community in a corporation-constructed neighbourhood located in a major city of the nation. It was built to house his almost 10,000 employees, for which they paid him rent. Using this position of power he controlled their lives (to be fired meant losing your home as well as your job). From this position of power, he imposed norms of behaviour with which they had to comply. Another example arrived a few years later, in 1893, on the other side of the ocean – this from the son of the founder of a large chocolate company. He conceived and constructed a 'Model Village'. It provided low-density housing, open space and gardens, for workers. This was all under a paternal regime based on the company owner's Quaker faith, which he used to create religiously inspired benign capitalism and a moral, alcohol-free village. At the time, drinking chocolate (cocoa) was promoted by Quakers as the moral substitute for alcohol and as such an enabler of abstinence.

De Santo took such ideas, modernised and upscaled them. Unlike the people around him, he saw the end of Cavarone as the beginning of an opportunity. Looking for a place for it to land, he spotted a small city in the desert just a fifty-minute drive due west. He hit its City Council with an offer they could not refuse: a half a billion-dollar plus investment if the city renamed it as Las Venus and gave him free licence to develop it. He would build two casinos, two nightclubs, a five-star motel and a restaurant cluster. He assured the Council that this catalytic action would draw a lot more investors. It did.

A year before Cavarone started to get seriously inundated, all but a few hundred of its once population of 3,200 remained. The city stood in silence awaiting its fate. De Santo had his deal. For a few hundred thousand, he bought what was once six of the prime properties of the strip. He had an idea – to create his Las Venus nightclubs and his motel from material extracted from them. The aim: to theme them as second-life – 'the Cavarone echo' as attractors to the 'old crowd'. He had already acquired all the client data from the businesses he bought. The publicity De Santo's project generated not only created a lot of interest; it also, again as he said it would, attracted people to move to the 'newborn city'. The pitch: 'come while rent are low and property prices cheap'; and 'if you're looking for construction work, or waiting for the job in a "hot" service industry then Las Venus is the place to be.'

Turge

The city engineer, Berndt Helvas, had directed the raising of the dike wall twice. It was now structurally impossible for it to go higher. Based on current data, the projection was that the rising sea level would top it in between seven and ten years. The City Council commissioned an internationally highly regarded engineer to review the conclusion that Helvas had reached. He duly confirmed that the city engineer was correct. As a result, the Council immediately banned any further construction in the city and announced it would begin a planned city relocation process. This would start with a public information campaign and a series of consultative public meetings, as well as the formation of a number of critical issues committees representing the key interests of the community, business, industry, education and health, as well as one created to search for a relocation destination – with representatives from the federal and state governments in the areas of housing, industry, employment and finance, as well as the chairperson from each of the city committees.

After four years, a low inundation risk relocation site was found, and the move process commenced. There were significant economic problems: the cost was high, and the loss of cash flow for businesses and industry was a serious issue that would have required transitional means of support, the temporary suspension of loan repayment and income assistance for essential employees while they were unable to work – this did not happen. There were many other social challenges and problems to resolve, especially for older members of the community, particularly for those with disabilities. Notwithstanding difficulties, progress was made on the staged new construction and moving programme. Two central housing areas were created and began to be populated, the creation of a central business district was well advanced and the establishment of a small commercial and retail sector was underway. Two schools were built, three of the eight major buildings of a university were nearing completion and construction work on the hospital was progressing. However, it was expected that the relocation would not be complete for another two years.

By this time, the old city was starting to have problems. The more the move progressed, the more dysfunctional it became, and the harder life became for those people yet to move. Concern about the state of the dike was growing. When it breaks, the expectation is that the nation will lose approximately 26 per cent of its productive agricultural land. The loss is aimed to be offset by fish-farming and seaweed cultivation as animal feedstock.

One event changed the picture and plans. A crack appeared in the dike. To relieve pressure, it was decided to release water into a wetland immediately. At the same time, an emergency relocation plan, part of an existing contingency action strategy, was initiated. This included creating emergency temporary accommodation and storage in the new city and immediately moving a large portion of the remaining community. The process took seven weeks; it was chaotic, generated a great deal of friction within and between the movers and those already moved. But it was exactly the right thing to do. Five weeks after this, the crack in the dike opened, much of the wall was washed away and the land submerged. Within a few days, the nation lost tens of thousands of hectares of agricultural land.

CALATTA

There is a long history of cities being built in stupid places, such as at the bottom of volcanoes, on floodplains, on earthquake fault lines or on hillsides in areas prone to landslides. Dominantly, this is done for reasons of economic expediency. The danger is known, but immediate economic benefits push concerns for risk aside.

Calatta is one of these cities. It is a delta port, and the city is built on silt. This means its foundations are structurally unsound. Silt soils are loose, and water flows through them, washing away finer particles. This is especially when heavy rain increases the volume and velocity of the river water flowing into the delta. As a result, settlement occurs, and the city starts to sink. Building footings and foundations become unstable. In turn, the lowered level of the city increases the risk of flooding. Many of these cities are in poorer nations, and the poorer sections are usually in the areas most likely to be flooded. This was certainly the case with Calatta. Just over 50 per cent of the city is informal, poor and in most years, it floods.

With a combination of sea level rises, more violent storms and more frequent floods, the situation has gotten increasingly worse. Many of the larger old buildings have become unstable and have had to be buttressed to prevent them from falling and closing. Even so, this has not prevented a few of them from doing so. Currently, the city is sinking half a metre per year. It is as if the city were disappearing in slow motion. People are worried. Those with money are drifting away, as are some businesses. This is making the poor and the city poorer. The need for the City Council to take action continually increases, but the ability to do so declines as the tax base of the city falls; thus, the financial means needed to take action simply do not exist. Exactly how long it will be before the critical condition of the city turns into a disaster is hard to tell because it depends on the frequency of extreme weather events. The general expectation from informed sources is that Calatta has five to ten years of life left before it dies in pain. As such, it will join a current trend of such cities around the world. One might expect that the Council would have made plans for evacuation and the establishment of evacuation shelters, along with accompanying food provision and medical support. But enquiries have found no evidence that this is the case. It seems that stupidity was present at the birth of the city and is equally present as it moves towards its death.

KANISKA

The City Government, like many others, was deeply concerned about sea level rises for two reasons: inundation and the flight of capital. On the first, and at great expense, they heightened the sea wall, raised street levels and had two pumping stations installed. What they did not tell the people of the city was that these actions and associated works were also about increasing the ability to evacuate the city quickly. Raised streets would not stop seawater getting into the city, including the retail areas. In fact they would trap it in a significant number of areas, hence the need for the pumping stations. The second concern is directly linked to the first. All the preventive works were as much about reassuring local capital that their property was being protected. The reality was, notwithstanding the expenditure, the actual protection gained would be minimal.

The city was home to one of the largest defence contractors in the nation, two electrical equipment companies, plus a large manufacturer of office furniture. Local government members obviously recognised that the flight of these organisations, the loss of revenue to the city and the resulting unemployment of many thousands of workers would be economically devastating. They viewed the economic danger as equal to that of rising sea levels. Thus, the government found itself in a double bind. It had to do something to reassure capital and the corporations, as well as taking action against the rising sea, while knowing that in the end the sea would win. The issue was how much time they could buy before this inevitability arrived. An unspoken reality of the action taken by the City Government was that a significant amount of it was actually cosmetic – a sign that something was being done just to reassure local capital and the city's population. In truth, it was clearly an act of deception.

The evidence from the research they commissioned from an international consultant, which they immediately locked away, was that the city would be flooded by inflow from the floodplain to its north. This land was already becoming salinated. The city's sea defences extended over less than 20 kilometres – eight to the north and twelve to the south. Whereas the defences needed to protect against floodplain inundation from the sea and the inlets of two rivers that ran to the south would not only have to extend over 50 kilometres, they would also require massive land purchases. They did not have the money, nor the means to acquire it, and even if they did, their income would be insufficient to repay a massive loan. The City Government also knew the state government would not be the major funder because this would open demand from many other cities with similar needs. The reality that they knew would eventually arrive, and have to be faced, would be the relocation of the city. But once this became general knowledge, the place would be doomed. Capital would flee, property values would collapse and the city would be worthless. Only three politicians knew and talked about this fate between themselves – the mayor, and the ministers of finance and environment. Other politicians had only been given a doctored executive summary of the consultant's report. Discussion was managed by the mayor and was muted. No doubt most of the elected representatives had reached the same conclusion, but somehow a conspiracy of silence formed. They just hoped that they would have left office before this situation became obvious and had to be confronted. Meanwhile, the mayor instructed the minister for the environment to work in secret on developing a relocation contingency plan.

LIMAN

People started leaving the city in numbers five years ago. By then it was clear the battle against rising sea levels was going to fail. As is always the case everywhere, it was the people with money and options who left first. Up until four months ago, people continued to leave: some with hope for their future, many in a state of despair. Most weeks, 5,000 to 10,000 people left. In the end, the sea forced even the poor and the desperate to leave. The sight was tragic: a few battered trucks, the odd old car with boxes and parcelled-up belongings strapped to the roof; then there were a few horse-drawn carts, but mostly hand carts and bicycles with bags tied to them being pushed, and people walking carrying what they could. There were animals aplenty – birds in small cages, chickens in big ones; cats in boxes, dogs and goats on lengths of rope and the occasional cow and donkey led from a halter. Most tragic of all were the old and the sick resting by the roadside, some never to rise. The road led to Hanling, a large city 76 kilometres to the south. It was clear that it would be a miracle if even half of these people made it there.

People moved slowly, trailing back several kilometres. Loads were lightened, and the road became strewn with things abandoned: pots and pans, heavy boots, bundles of clothes, garden tools and toys that children were carrying and dropped. The further the distance, the greater the shedding, and the greater the numbers of the defeated and exhausted, the old and sick were left lying or sitting alone at the roadside.

Hanling knew a lot of people were coming. A detention camp had been set up 2 kilometres outside the city to prevent them from entering the city. Barricades had been placed across the road; and on either side stretching out several hundred metres were high-voltage electric fences powered by a towed generator. Behind the barricades were more than two hundred police officers dressed in riot gear. At their feet were a riot shield and a long baton hanging from their belt, along with a gas mask, tear-gas canisters and two stun grenades. The expected numbers had been grossly underestimated; 15,000 to 20,000 were expected, whereas 35,000 to 45,000 were on their way.

Over the journey, the column first strung out and then gradually divided into three cohorts: a thinly scattered collection of stragglers that included the old and the unfit; families travelling with large loads and with children finding it hard going, along with older, fitter people who did not move quickly but kept going; and then, the strutters who travelled light and covered twenty kilometres a day, making the journey in under five days. Those who struggled took seven days, and the stragglers took between nine and eleven days. Over two hundred died on the way.

The detention camp was divided into 5,000 lots on a grid of tent sites and pathways. At the end of the east, north and west paths were portable toilets and posts with taps connected to hoses. On each lot was a family-sized tent with a large white grid number stencilled onto it. Inside the tent was a black rubber bucket. The entrance was on the south side, and there was a reception area of ten marked-out queue lines, each with a registration table at the end. To the left was a large kitchen tent, and to the right a small medical tent. The way the camp had been organised and the electric perimeter fence made a large gathering impossible.

The strutters met as a group at the end of each day. They knew they would be attempted to be controlled and contained. They had a rough plan of action, which they would revise once they had a clearer picture of what to expect. They selected ten good runners to go ahead on the morning of day five. To get a view of what awaited them then, they would run back to report. Once they returned, the group would stop, meet and plan. Information from the runners indicated that the camp was not big enough for everyone on the road. In addition to an electric fence, it was surrounded by a large body of police. They talked for over an hour. A small group, all of whom had done military service, proposed a plan and put it to the group. It was supported.

The plan was based on the agreement that they did not want to be put in what looked like a detention camp, plus the families and the elderly were not in a position to resist, and they needed a place to rest, recover and in some cases get medical help. Based on this situation, the plan was for surprise and rapid action. There were about 5,000 strutters who would take action, knowing that a huge number of police were expecting trouble. So, the plan was to hit the police fast and hard. They would push the barricade back with a frontal strike, then two groups would rush in from the gaps at the sides. Within the left entry a group of twenty had been tasked to turn off and disable the generator. Everyone else would come in from the flanks to circle around behind the police and attack from the back, with another group of about twenty instructed to take out the police radio and command-and-control van as quickly as possible. Once the police had been overwhelmed, zip cuff the police with their own cuffs that they all carry. Speed and surprise were to be their weapons.

Things didn't go exactly to plan. The police struck before the charge at the barricade. They realised they were totally outnumbered, knew they were going to be attacked and hoped to 'cut off the head of the snake' before it could bite. They failed. The strike force absorbed the attack and the rest of the group divided and acted as instructed. It was all more chaotic than planned, but the intended end result was attained. The police had underestimated the level of organised resistance.

Some people were gassed. They were taken to the taps to wash their eyes. The general instruction was to scatter in groups and aim for tree cover. All but a few did this. Police helicopters would be in the air quickly. By this time it was late afternoon; people stayed undercover until dark, then travelled under the cover of darkness and headed for the city lights.

Again, they had a plan: as soon as it got dark, they would come together, and then split into two groups: one travelling east, one west for two hours and then due south. The aim was to enter the city in small groups from the east, south and west rather than directly from the north. As individuals, these men and women were free national subjects who had committed no crime other than resisting containment by the police on that day. Together they had been designated as a dangerous mass representing a threat to the city.

When the families arrived at the camp, it was clear that it was too small, that the whole reception process was in a mess, there had been conflict and that action had to be taken before the old and sick arrived. The NGO organisers realised this. As a result, women and children were bused, under protest, to two hostels and four church halls. Two days later, the men were moved to the empty army reserve barrack. Four more days later, a tented family centre was opened in the city park.

Over the next three months, an already existing but underdeveloped relocation programme of placing families camped in Hanling in other cities was implemented. The strutters relocated themselves, many getting buses and trains out of the city on the first day of their arrival, while others stayed with people they knew; some stayed and started looking for work. If there was any police effort to round them up, it was half hearted – they knew a significant number had already left the city and tracking down the rest would take considerable police resources. As for the old and sick, a field hospital under canvas was set up in the grounds of the City General Hospital. All were examined. Some were admitted into hospital and aged care facilities in Hanling and other cities. The majority stayed back in the reception camp, which was improved and equipped for them. Within a year, temporary accommodation was installed in the camp, this with the effect of it transitioning to a 'retirement village' albeit at its the absolute most basic form.

HANLING – A LIMAN POSTSCRIPT

The number and scale of destroyed cities and population displacements put these issues on the global political agenda with an unavoidable presence. In recognition of this, an 'international crisis forum' was held in Hanling. It was selected for the event because of its proximity to the world's most recent disaster in Liman, the human consequences of which were still very evident in the city.

The event was attended by Ministers of Disaster from one hundred and twenty governments internationally, and representatives of many disaster-focused NGOs. On paper, a great deal was achieved over the five days. A resolution was presented and adopted on: globally mapping cities at risk within a year; the need to establish a 'global population agency with a clearly defined contingency action-plans to manage displaced populations agreed to be formed and funded'. Dovetailing with this was a stated requirement for cities at risk to have an annually reviewed population evacuation and distribution plan to counter the organic formation of a mono-directional mass on the move. This plan also needed to deal with the problem of 'late leavers'. All this was the easy bit. The hard part was getting the money for a central emergency relief fund and establishing its means of implementation. One related action was agreed – the secure stockpiling of emergency transportable resources in critical materials areas (like plastic sheeting, tent poles, rope, tools, bottled water and food concentrates) able to be air-dropped quickly to where they were needed in the immediate aftermath of a disaster. One year was allocated to put this and all the other agreed measures in place, and to resolve those without agreement.

The last day of the event was an informal buffet lunch to which fifty elderly and injured people from Liman were invited. All these individuals were from a field hospital in Hanlin. There were fifty tables, each with a Liman person sitting at it, each being invited to tell their story to the delegates. It worked well at most tables, but for a few of them, the challenge was too much.

While some progress was made at the event, it was not enough. Most nations pleaded for more time. Predictably, climate impact events travelled at a faster speed than the response to them. The model of humanitarian 'help' was just not capable of meeting the continuing and growing crisis. Clearly, intervention after a disaster could not, and would not, be adequate. As critics of the whole disaster management approach made clear, based on risk data, the priority was intervention before the disaster. The point of such intervention was to assist, enable and facilitate communities to gain the practical, material, psychological and economic means to deal with it themselves. As many delegates recognised and acknowledged, for the vast majority of communities, the inevitable outcome now unfolding was that their only source of help would be from themselves. The speed and scale of climate impacts that will arrive are going to completely overwhelm the capability of all governments and NGOs' ability to respond.

In this respect, events like an 'international crisis forum' were out of touch. Action, defined by historical experience, has to be proactive, not reactive. This means that addressing disaster events actually needs to be directed towards recognising the conditions of change in time and giving warnings. Thereafter, the role of governments and NGOs should be prefigurative and focused on coping assistance based on all available means. The unspoken consensus was that this is the face of reality.

Flood

SURINO

Famed for its horticultural economy, especially its potatoes, the region around Surino was irrigated by glacial melt run-off and summer rain. This had been for as long as history had been written and stories had been told. But then the climate started to change. It became warmer, and the environment and life began to transform. At first, things improved, plenty of sun and more water meant the land was even more productive. But with more sun and the continued melting of glacial ice, more water became too much. There were floods, and each year they got worse. Then came the great flood. It had been especially hot, and water was pouring off the glacier. Then there were massive storms. An enormous amount of water flowed across the fertile plain with great force. Everything was washed away: crops, buildings, cars, roads, bridges, animals and people.

Where once there was the small city of Surino, villages and farms, now there was nothing but a sea of mud covering hundreds of square kilometres. The only people who survived were those who managed to flee from the torrent of water and then of mud. Tragically, there were only a few of them. The event not only erased the present of the region, it shaped its future. As in the most ancient world, the glacier would disappear, and the landscape would mark its lost presence. Another way of life would have to be created. But at the moment, its form remains completely unclear.

HAKI

It started raining on Monday; it was still raining on Sunday. The local radio station SXFM had issued its first flood warning at 5.00 p.m. It said that if the rain continued, there will have to be a major release of the Pamou dam to prevent it from overflowing. The rain did not stop.

Koji Nishima lived on the western edge of the city 4.5 kilometres from the dam. It was almost 6:30 on Monday night, and he and his wife were about to eat. Koji was washing his hands when he heard a distant roar. He had never heard it before, but he knew what it was.

Their daughter Aoi Nishima was getting ready for work; this was only her second week as assistant manager at the London branch of the Mizuhi SK Bank. She had made her lunch, but her phone was still charging and she still needed to clean her shoes. There was no rush. She was finishing her coffee and half-watching the news, but then: 'The Asian city of Haki has been drowned as a result of the walls of the city's dam bursting.'

. . .

Along with several thousand other people, Aoi was standing on the banks of a lake. Beneath it lay the city of her birth, her parents, other members of her family, friends and over one hundred thousand other people who had resided there – aunts, uncles, school friends and all the others who had populated her life.

Some people were laying photographs on the water; others threw an object into the water – a toy, a piece of jewellery, a key – but mostly people just laid a flower. Aoi's was red, her mother's favourite colour. Lots of people were crying, some silently, others audibly. She just sat near the water, hugging her knees. Her eyes were closed, and she was lost in memories. It was not until she got back to the hire car that she realised she had been by the lake for over four hours. She drove to the airport, hoping she could get a flight back to London.

Grief overwhelmed all other emotions. The feeling of loss was unbounded. Himrau, her cousin and, besides her, the only other family still alive, phoned from Peru while Aoi was queuing at Heathrow for a taxi. For the past five years, he had been working there as an eye doctor. He had got the news and had made many calls, with no response. They talked briefly, and Himaru said he would come to see her as soon as he could get away.

Landslide

PAMPOLOS

Scores of cities around the country were flooded during the past year, but Pampolos suffered the worst. This was not just because the water rose to the rooftops of thousands of single-storey homes, but because a landslide from a mountain at either end of the valley had cut the city off. Now to the north there was a wall of rock and earth that was 140 metres wide, over 25 metres high, and over a 100 metres deep, while to the south, a storm-water culvert under the road had blown. As a result, rushing water under pressure cut an ever-larger channel that washed away the earth and rock under the road. The result was that the road collapsed. The more water that raged through the channel, the deeper it got. In the end, it was over 40 metres wide and 12 metres deep. The road had also been washed out in three other places lower down, although not nearly as badly.

As days passed, the crisis in the city deepened. The water and power had been cut. There were some houses with tanks of water. There was bottled water in supermarkets and other retail outlets, but due to the flood, it was mostly not reachable. All sources of water, other than the bottled water, were required to be boiled. This was only possible for houses with bottled gas available, but the supply was again limited by flooding. A lot of fresh food was either damaged, contaminated or both. All the supermarkets, but one, had been flooded. Sixty percent of all homes were badly flooded. A few escaped without flood damage, but the majority, just under 40 per cent, had one metre or less of inundation.

Many people cut off by high water for a day without any foreseeable prospect of rescue, no food, or any means to boil water, drank the flood water knowing, or not, that it was contaminated with sewage.

No help of any kind arrived until the early morning of day two. This arrived in the form of multiple flights of air-dropped small inflated rubber boats filled with plastic packs of bottled water and high-energy food bars taped to their sides. An emergency response team was helicoptered in to assess the city's situation. The team, two civil and structural engineers, a public health doctor, a logistics specialist and a videographer, had two inflatables with outboards. They were instructed to make an initial report to the National Minister for Emergencies and Disaster Relief by the end of the day.

THEIR REPORT IN BRIEF

An on-site command and control centre needs to be immediately established. The situation is grave. The city's population of 110,000 people is at high risk. There have been fatalities. The numbers are unknown, but likely to be in the hundreds. People are hungry, thirsty, sick and getting worse quickly. Cholera has already broken out. Within a few days, people will start to die. Both hospitals are flooded and are struggling to deal with their own situation. The landslide to the north has impeded flood water drainage and increased the back-up of water in the city. Water levels are falling very slowly. The crisis will remain extreme for at least a week. There are only small pockets of dry land in the south of the city. There are only a dozen or so small boats in the city, plus those air-dropped in. The distribution of food and water needs dramatic support and improvement.

Pathfinding teams are needed to plot and mark existing routes. Water depths vary; walkout routes when viable, have to be used. It would take too long to evacuate by boat. Lifejackets are required and should be made available and issued to walkers. Water police would be appropriate in conjunction with local police. Marking should be done using provided fluorescent paint spray.

The condition of the population is fair to poor and deteriorating. Time is of the essence.

It is recommended that the city be evacuated urgently. This cannot be done by air. It could only be considered by heavy-lift helicopters, but few are available; their carrying capacity is too low, the number of people too large and getting people to the assembly point too complex. At present, there is no possible way to exit from the south,

Evacuation has to be from the north. This involves 110,000 adults and children in need of food and water. To achieve this, a path through the landslide has to be created. The recommendation is that two large dozers, trucked in from the south, create a path over its top. However, getting people in number to its entry point will be very hard. It will require a significant number of Zodiacs (rubber boats with outboards) and the use of all available small boats to ferry people to this point. Even when operating for extensive periods daily, it will take days. Additionally, airlift medevac extraction would be needed

Reception teams would be needed to greet arrivals with hot soup and blankets. Medical assistance would also be needed at this point of arrival. All-wheel-drive ambulances would likewise be needed at the arrival point to transport the sick. Help for the elderly and physically disabled to walk to bus transport would also be required.

Once over the landslide, a large-scale mass transportation capability needs to be immediately organised. The establishment of emergency evacuation centres is required as near as possible to the departure point so that as many people as possible can be moved in a circular system. Ambulances and hospital care would be needed for several thousand (command centre estimates being gained as soon as possible).

Contingency planning to speed the draining of the city and its restoration to function post-evacuation should commence as soon as is feasible. To enable this, a temporary work camp should be established to the south of the city, and as near as possible to it. The city public works department and its fire department – with hired or recovered equipment – should be early occupants and assist in draining and cleaning the city. Thereafter, the state governments, with federal assistance, need to establish a construction evaluation group to work with insurance assessment teams, a social services support team, and a finance and economic recovery group to scope the level of assistance needed. It could be expected that the rehabilitation of the city will take up to three years.

The immediate need is to secure the city – by remote monitoring and a police response capability.

They concluded: 'What we have submitted is done on the basis that action has to be taken immediately. The rate of death can be expected to rapidly accelerate within three days.'

A full report was submitted seven days after the first that confirmed that the evacuation was successful, reported on fatalities and casualties, the location and numbers of people in evacuation centres, and progress on the clean-up, as well as a technical inspection of the city. Plans by utility companies to reconnect the city, and from the Department of Roads to clear and reconstruct roads were indicated to be forthcoming. The expectation is that these works would take many months, and major structural work in the city would not commence until services and road connections were restored.

The report indicated that prior to this recent event, the city had no history of major flood events. While this recent event appears to be a freak occurrence, the now changed and changing, climate conditions indicate that historical data cannot be viewed as normative. Prior to a major expenditure on the restoration of the city, the report recommended that a full risk assessment of the city be undertaken and that the form of future action not be considered until this review is complete and has been considered. It also recommended that the City Council be reformed in exile. The city and its population must be consulted and empowered so as to have full involvement in the nature and form of the restoration of the city.

ASTRAVILLE

The story of Astraville is one of an old city and its destruction by a new one – Harridorf.

Astraville was a service city for lowland farming communities, the majority of which owned dairy farms with cattle that thrived on the rich pastures of this area's temperate region. Harridorf was a new city built on a plateau at the top of hills that directly rose in the west behind Astraville. It was created to service the new hydraulic fracturing industry extracting natural gas from rocky areas deep in the earth. The resource extended across the entire western plains. A huge incision had been cut into the hill for a highway to enable Harridorf to be constructed and to connect the city to Astraville. All the plant and equipment needed for the industry were carried on this highway, as well as the material needed to service the new city. Running alongside it was the pipe installed to carry the liquefied gas to the port of Rhein and to awaiting tankers – this capability represented a large investment in the industry and two hundred kilometres of a steel gas pipeline.

The storm was forecast well in advance. Storms were common in the region and usually welcomed. Their rain keeps the grass growing, its nutrient level high, and so the cows' milk continues to flow. But this storm was different. Not only was the rain very heavy, but it continued for a very long time. The result was over 560 millimetres of rain in 36 hours. That is a lot of rain. The result was devastating. The run-off from the hard landscape surfaces of the new city meant a huge torrent of water rushing down the hillside. The whole area above Astraville had been cleared of trees during the construction of the winding road, so there was nothing to slow the water's downward velocity. Increasingly, the river turned from water to mud. It travelled towards the city, carrying rocks that once, with tree roots, had held topsoil in place. The weight, speed and the surface tension of this mass meant a great slab of the hillside was loosened, fell away and then slid ever faster down it, heading for the old city below.

The city, with its fine old timber buildings, beautiful city park, heritage theatre and courthouse were all gone in less than an hour. Fragments of smashed buildings and battered vehicles appeared in the monotone environment of rocks and mud that now covered the city. Not only had the material form of the city gone, but also its life. Neither would return.

The inquiry into the cause of the disaster concluded the absolutely obvious – blame rested with the design, form and amount of hard landscape of the new city, with the people who hired and directed the contractors to remove all the trees on the hillside, the builders and road makers who failed to establish sufficient storm-water drainage. When confronted with these findings, the architects, designers, contractors, builders and Harridorf Council claimed *force majeure*. No legal action was taken.

The overwhelming view across the state was that Astraville should be rebuilt. However, it would not be possible to renew what had been lost, but there was a strong view that a new city should reflect the materials and spirit of the old city, but not be built on it. The state government also required Harridorf to retrofit the hard landscape and, in doing so, enable ground water absorption, and install the means to detain and retain run-off. Likewise, the contractor had the choice of replanting the hillside with advanced saplings or defending themselves against legal action for removing trees that should have been preserved: they replanted. There was a consensus that the disaster should never be repeated. A lake was created to the east of what would become New Astraville, as well as a key element of a catchment management scheme to capture future hill run-off; it was also a place of pleasure and leisure. It was named twelve-forty-seven to mark the twelve hundred and forty-three adults and four children who lost their lives in the landslide.

CASSAN

Once the City of Cassan was a fishing village. A trace of its past still exists in the small number of fishing boats that still work out of its harbour, as well as more than a dozen charter boats of various sizes. Their business: wealthy tourists who hire them, and their crew, for a day to a week's fishing. However, the fame and the economy of the city did not come from the sea, but from the fine clay that was found at the base of the hills that loomed over the city just to its south. Who knows when it was discovered, but it was long before there were any written records. What is known is that the city from ancient times had been celebrated for its potters and their pottery. There are many beautiful pieces from these times in the city museum.

By the early nineteenth century, there was still traditional pot making, but there was also the start of industrially produced ceramics. It was this industry that made the city grow, become well-known and rich.

To expand, the city had to reclaim land from the sea. It did this by blasting rock out of the cliffs at the water's edge, and then pushing it into the sea, slowly extending the shoreline. Thereafter, building the level up and then backfilling. By this means, and over a period of five years, 9,000 square metres of land were created to build on. Over time, most of the hills behind the city had been cleared of trees to produce charcoal as fuel for the kilns. As the topsoil was washed away, the hill directly behind the city ceased to be green and was just bare rock. House construction started at the base of the cliffs as the reclaimed area was stabilised and levelled.

As the city grew in size, so did its economy and population. To deal with the demand for housing, high-rise apartments were built; this being much cheaper than land reclamation, as more land from the sea would have been very expensive. During this period, major improvements to the coastal road were made.

. . .

It started raining on the last day of summer. At first, it was gentle and welcome; it hadn't rained for months. After ten days, it had not stopped. Then, on day eleven it got really heavy; days twelve and thirteen were even worse, as was day fourteen. At 8:10 a.m., soil and rocks started to pour over the historically formed erosion at the base of the rock wall. Coming down the rock face at speed, rocks smashed into more than twenty houses, causing extensive damage. Meanwhile, the earth turned to mud and started to flow into the city. At 3:00 a.m. on day fifteen, there was a massive rockfall. It sounded like the end of the world. Not only were houses smashed to pieces and some of their occupants killed, but three 28-storey tower blocks were destroyed. Nothing escaped damage. Eight hundred and forty lives were lost, and 221 people were rescued. All of them were badly injured – nine of them were children. There were many more with minor injuries. Sent in by the government, a team of geologists and engineers arrived at 1:15 in the afternoon of day seventeen to inspect the situation. They installed sensors and measuring equipment and said it would take several days to initially assess the situation. But what they could say was that it was serious and dangerous and that the city should be evacuated until the situation was clear.

Within four hours, the government had ordered this to be done by sea as the coastal road was blocked. Evacuation was conducted by three ferries, four navy assault landing craft and a hospital ship, and commenced as soon as the vessels arrived. Helicopters had already taken most seriously injured individuals to hospitals. In the afternoon, people were removed from the most exposed areas. The next morning, the process of evacuation began in earnest. All the vessels were present. The evacuation commenced day and night over two days, and 46,756 adults and children from the city were taken to a tented evacuation centre created at Port Murelle by the army, 26 kilometres down the coast. By late afternoon on day two of the evacuation, it was complete.

It took twelve days for the government to receive the inspection report. In summary, it said the situation was unstable, and to make it safe, it would require blasting unsafe areas of the cliff, earthworks and work at its top, and then substantial engineering works to make the base of the hill safe and to create a safe containment zone. This would take at least one year. Before this commenced, the coastal road had to be cleared, the city needed to be made safe and damaged buildings repaired, and new ones constructed. This was to be done with the help of a team of building owners, engineers and construction companies. The city would be divided into two zones: Zone One, waterfront and city centre; Zone Two, industrial hill facing suburbs. Nobody could return until the blasting was complete, and significant areas of the city were made inhabitable. These works were expected to take seven months. Once done, people in Zone One with livable homes and business premises could return. Once the safety construction works were advanced, people from Zone Two could return if they had undamaged property. To clear fallen rock, a major land reclamation project would commence. People whose homes had been lost, and where defence structures would be built, would be offered homes on newly created reclaimed land. This would take two years. The planning of temporary accommodation would be provided in the meantime.

A committee of representatives from banks, the insurance industry and the government departments of finance and housing was formed to address issues with insurance claims, financial support for displaced families and business owners, temporary accommodation and the creation of a national donation fund. Finally, the government announced the establishment of a board of inquiry to examine the circumstances of the accident with unrestricted terms of reference. It also announced that a garden of commemoration would be built for all who lost their lives, and the city would be renamed New Cassan.

Rinmirer

First, a picture.

This city is a small city, 1400 metres above sea level in the Bulinera mountains. It was created to service the Serrea corporation's coal 'mountain top removal mining project'. Besides excavating the top of the mountain, they also built a pelleting plant to turn coal dust into a product. The whole operation employs more than 4,000 workers. The extracted coal was taken by trucks to the rail head 20 kilometres from the base of the mountain. The mine also created employment for more than a thousand other workers, including mechanics servicing the conveyors, bucket excavators, dump trucks, medics, caterers, school teachers and people working in retail. Together with all the other businesses in the city and public services, plus families, the population of this small city is just over 20,000 people.

The operation started thirty-five years ago and, to date, it has taken about 150 metres off the top of the mountain. It has attracted a lot of bad press for pumping huge volumes of water from a river near the base of the mountain. The coal-wash run-off, which cut a channel down the side of the mountain, caused an enormous amount of biological damage and also polluted the river. Atmospheric emissions from the engines of pumps, extraction machinery and of a constant stream of trucks driving up and down the mountain road every day contribute to the problem. Then there is the dust from the mine settling on the city of Karrina at the base of the mountain, which has created appalling public health problems.

At the beginning of the year, the mountain range was hit by a series of severe storms. Heavy rain continued for weeks. The mine filled with water and overflowed down the drainage channel. The run-off etched away the road base and soil underneath it. All this was made worse by the extensive tree clearing done during road construction. A section of the road was gone, and with it, a whole segment of the side of the mountain covered the road. Twelve hours later, the gap in the road was 80 metres, and a landslide at the base of the mountain covered a large section of the road.

The city and the mine were now stranded by an unbridgeable gap. The mountain had taken its revenge. In the space of a few hours, the once functional city had become stranded and awaited the imminent departure of life.

The only way to get people out was by heavy-lift helicopters. With help from the army and three private companies flying up to ten flights a day to Karrina, it took eight days to evacuate the city's population, where a reception centre had been set up, and from which people were transported to a number of evacuation centres in the country. Each person had been permitted to carry one small bag that they could place on their lap. For several weeks after the evacuation, a team from the mining company and four hired heavy-lift helicopters recovered some equipment, vehicles and smaller items from the medical centre and offices that were parked in the transport yard they owned, and the warehouse they rented in Karrina.

The government ordered an enquiry, which took eighteen months. It concluded that while it was technically possible to bridge the gap in the road and clear and repair it, the cost would be considerable. However, a risk assessment had concluded that the event causing the destruction is likely to be repeated given the current and expected climatic conditions. It therefore recommended that the mine be abandoned and that the city and road be destroyed, and the mountainside be replanted with trees, if possible. This was all to prevent run-off from the hard surfaces causing a repeated disaster during an extreme weather event. Rejecting opposition from the mining company, the government accepted the recommendation and ordered the Army Corps of Engineers to demolish what remained of the road by explosion. It also opened a tender for a major tree replanting project.

Everyone was in financial trouble: homeowners, medium and small businesses and the large corporations. Nobody had insurance against what was deemed to be *force majeure* – this a specified clause in insurance policies and contracts that removes liability for an 'act of God'. However, at a cost, it is possible to insure against some natural disasters. *But nobody had a policy that covered the destruction of the highway and the landslide. The only possibility was a class action against the road construction company. However, this was not pursued, as even if they had been found liable, they would not have had the funds to meet costs of hundreds of millions.*

Heat

It had been dry for months. Last year was the same, and also the year before. Expecting this situation to continue, Daniel had put in four new 244,000 litre water tanks. To fill them, he added a lean-to on the south of the house with a 65 by 5 metre polycarbonate roof, to increase the volume of rainwater caught. Each tank also had its own funnel catcher. He also added two more 10 by 100 high-tinted polytunnels to the six he already had built. Growing crops in the open had been impossible for years.

Daniel's market garden was 12 kilometres from the city. He and his wife Carol bought it twenty-three years ago and they ran it together until she died of heat-induced heart failure, due to an existing condition, four years ago at the age of fifty-six. Everything they had created was designed to be 'stand alone': water, power, sewage were all independent systems. For two decades, an income had been earned from growing tomatoes, beans, lettuce, cucumbers, radishes, shallots, strawberries and blueberries. Pollinators now lived in the polytunnels, attracted by companion flower planting. Bees especially like this environment; it helps them survive.

. . .

Today was the last day of the city. Almost everyone had already left, three-quarters of them relocating to Krester, a new city in the Southern Highlands four hundred and 80 kilometres away. The mayor, who had stayed to the last, was meeting a film crew arriving mid-morning. They were making a documentary on the end of the city and the work of the contractors who had been hired to demolish it and recover reusable material. They would be working from late afternoon to midnight, half this time under lights. It was too hot to work in the open during the day. Some structures would be carefully disassembled, but most would be ripped apart and then whatever was left standing would be knocked over with a bulldozer. Occasionally, a solid structure would be demolished using Semtex explosives. The contractors had several materials teams with special equipment. The materials – concrete (crushed), recovered timber (de-nailed), metals (especially iron, steel, copper, aluminium, lead and brass), and rubber and plastics – all materials were organised into three inventories: reusable components (from doors and windows to roof trusses and water tanks), reusable materials (crushed concrete, timber, copper, steel and plastic pipe), and toxic and biodegradable disposables.

By law, every abandoned city had to recycle all recyclables and recover all materials that had reusable value. Thereafter, the site of the city had to be levelled, made environmentally safe and a sign, no smaller than 2 by 6 metres, erected in materials that would endure, stating the name of the city, the year it was founded and ended, plus the size of its population prior to the decision to relocate.

. . .

Daniel knew Rolando, the mayor, well. They had gone to school together and played in the same soccer team when they were young men. They rarely socialised together but took their friendship as a given fact of their lives. When they met just before the destruction of the city started, they merely shook hands. Everything that could be said about the fate of the city had already been said. They watched in silence as the contractors started to go about their business.

Daniel could have moved with the city, but he opted to stay where he was. He had invested in his means of survival. It was where he wanted to be. He didn't feel too old to start over again, just too sad. Every day, at some moment, he would wander over to Carol's grave and have a conversation with her. Where she was laid to rest is where she would stay, and thus he was going nowhere.

Besides the upkeep of the water and the tunnels, he had other plans. He would enlarge his solar array so he could put in more cold storage. He also wanted to get a better-used electric truck with a longer range and a cold box. Now that Loree was gone, he had to take his produce to the market at Junnor, which was eighty kilometres away. His existing truck could do it, but only just. He wanted to get home immediately after unloading and not spend time recharging. The other issue was labour. In the past, he could hire a casual worker from Loree when he needed help. Now he would have to employ someone who would live there. This meant making part of the house into a self-contained unit. With the extra tunnels increasing his productivity, he could afford a modest wage. He thought he would first start with an overseas student on a working visa. He also thought about himself. He didn't want to be a hermit. His social life was not much since Carol died. Most weeks he would go into Loree for a beer on a Friday night. He always bumped into someone he knew. That was now the past. Thinking about the future, he liked the idea of passing knowledge onto, and talking with, a young person.

Daniel looked forward to taking his weekly produce load to the new market. But he missed the local weekly paper. The Junnor paper would be full of people, places and events to which he had no connection, so he would not bother to buy it. He thought about the future a lot. He was sixty-seven. He was sure he had a saleable business; food production was a high-demand industry, although it would take a while to sell. He would give it another ten years. He did not exactly know where he would go, except that after all this heat and dryness he wanted to live somewhere near water and cool nights. He pictured a cottage by the sea. But then there was Carol. Most nights he read for an hour or so. He treasured his bookcase. He had maybe a hundred books, all old. He just kept reading them. One of his favourites was Ernest Hemingway's *The Old Man and the Sea*. It was this book that gave him a dream of living by the sea and catching a big fish. He had never done any fishing, but one day, if he lived by the sea, he would. Anyway, it was a good dream. Would he stay? Would he go? Time would tell.

Usakia

Like an increasing number of cities, Usakia has been killed by
heat and drought. Economically destroyed and made unviable and
unliveable by heat, the city was abandoned. Some homes and businesses were secured by their owners in the hope that they would be
able to return one day when the climate had improved. Most factories had their machinery removed by their owners. Almost all businesses were boarded up.

The exodus from the city spanned two years. Within the first
year, the population dropped from 84,790 to 36,224. In that year, it
was obviously mostly the people who could easily move who left: the
young, the unencumbered and the financially mobile. The rest hung
on in the hope that things would change, but they did not. Most left
of their own accord. Some had to be removed, but not forcefully. A
very few barricaded themselves in their homes and were removed by
force. Seventeen ended their own lives rather than move.

Besides the unbearable climatic conditions, once the utility companies moved out there was no water, power or gas. Likewise, there
were no medical services, police, fuel or functioning shops. Within
a few weeks, illegal wrecking contractors arrived, set up camps and
started to strip the place. Doors, windows, timber, roofing sheets,
copper pipes – anything easy to remove, transport and stockpile was
fair game. No effort by anybody was made to stop them. Such activity was common and happening nationwide. Meanwhile, the people who moved headed for cities in the north where it was cooler.
This migration was happening from all over the south. The result
was that informal settlements started to proliferate in cities all over
the north – this enabled by the emergence of a huge boom in used
building materials businesses. Here was a perverse circular economy

where people were metaphorically, or even literally, buying things they once, and in some cases, still legally owned (like windows, doors and floorboards). All of this was being driven by whole armies of city wreckers. While all this was happening, people were living in tents and cars, and eating in soup kitchens.

Accompanying this chaotic process of transition and enviro-climatic disaster, there was a financial crisis. Defaults on mortgages, business loans, car loans and more were massive. The mechanisms of repossession were completely dysfunctional, as millions of people had no fixed address, and people simply took off, leaving their past lives behind them. They had one agenda; the only thing they had in mind was survival. They had whatever cash they could manage to muster, and they took any kind of job they could find to get an income, and took whatever roof over their heads and family they could find, make or afford. For the latecomers, the speed of the progression from a life of order to chaos was astounding.

One of the major expanding industries in this situation was security. Law and order were under enormous pressure. The structures of an organised and orderly society were quickly breaking down, as informal community growth rates exploded. The lived distinction between the legal and the illegal was blurring. Thievery was not only rampant but large-scale and structural, as seen with the wrecker companies. So, anyone with money who had anything of value that was visible – home, car, truck, boat, plane – who wanted to keep it hired security. Corruption was rife; violence could be but a few moments away. What for most people in most places was once a world of fictional dystopia in movies had become a lived reality.

The power of the state vanished as soon as it became bankrupt. It was replaced by local structures, a few good, but mostly bad. For a while, under the control of San Ho, the former mayor who had the city police force behind him, the city of Usakia was safe. The situation remained fine until members of the police force drifted away as numbers leaving increased. Chaos followed, and it dramatically accelerated the speed of departures, including Ho's.

VIOEDO

The people of the City of Vioedo were used to heat. There was shade: a square with trees and a fountain, a city park with a tree-lined avenue and shaded seats, awnings over shop fronts, plus two swimming pools, well-oriented, cross-ventilated homes, and air-conditioned malls, shops and workplaces. Even so, for several years, it has been getting hotter. Fifteen years ago, there were three or four days a year when it was over C45°, but now it's over thirty, with a few reaching over C50°. Now the hot city experiences killer heat. Old people are dying in this heat; babies are also dying in the womb and after being born.

The school day has been shortened; outdoor workers now start their day at 4:30 a.m. and finish at noon. Some work at night under lights. Crops are failing, trees are stressed and dying, and once green parks are now expanses of dust. There is no moisture in the soil at all. There is no grass or plant to be seen except where they are irrigated by wastewater. As for fresh water, it is rationed.

Four cities in the region have been designated by the Department of Health as uninhabitable. Their populations have been, or are being, relocated. If they refuse to move, they are arrested so the state cannot be held liable for death by their relatives. Everyone in Vioedo expects it to be the next city to be designated as unliveable. The City Council should have started to plan for relocation years ago. Everyone knows why this did not happen. There is now nowhere to relocate to. The small number of higher and cooler possible relocation sites have all now been occupied. People are leaving for these places. While not going anywhere, or turning to dust, the city is disappearing.

Drought

BENSON

In its heyday, Benson was a rough but wealthy oil city. People wanted to invest in the place, and they invested big. It could afford the best. This was exactly what the City Council wanted when it hired architect Andrew Jenson. He was young, but already rated as one, if not the most gifted architect in the country. He was thirty-four when he was appointed. His job brief was simply stated as a challenge: deliver a beautiful city. Even before he got the job, he knew how he would approach it. He would rebuild the city around a magnificent park. To create it, he would employ the famous landscape architect Johnathon Crabbe. This is exactly what he did. Like all Crabbe's work, it looked nice when it was completed, and amazing a decade later. The park attracted a lot of attention, not just because it was so good, but also because it was the last one Crabbe designed before he died. While oil was dark and dirty, what the city created from its money was light and clean.

The city Jensen delivered was elegant, and like the park, it became more so as it matured. But those days are long gone.

The oil was exhausted, and the money made from it not only produced a beautiful city but also one with a sound economy based on manufacturing. Two major corporations were lured to it. The first to come was the engineering corporation Cass and Weston, one of the nation's largest makers of machine tools. The second to arrive was the Holgate medical and surgical equipment company. They manufactured everything from hospital beds and operating tables to surgical instruments. For four decades, the city thrived; then fate stepped in, and the situation changed.

There had been many droughts in the state over the years. Drought was elemental to its environment and to history. But there had never been one in living memory, or recorded history, like this one. It started decades ago and remained ongoing. The reality is that rain is no longer part of its climate and bioregion. Climate change brought the city and the region a rainless desert. Climate scientists at the Weather Bureau confirmed this to be true. They knew long before this was publicly announced but were instructed to remain silent by the government. Businesses, including the big ones, and many people who worked for them, moved away. They did not wait for the city dam to run dry.

Money was spent by the Council looking for bore water. None was found. The beautiful city park became nothing but dead trees and dust. Once it was clear that the city would totally run out of water, property values, which had been declining for several years, completely crashed. Businesses that had been struggling to keep going closed, and most of the remaining people hung onto a faint hope that things would change. At this point, the City Council ordered a complete evacuation of the city.

In consultation with the City Council, the state sent in contractors to extract anything of material value from the city, such as usable building materials, quality furniture, operational machinery and recyclables, especially iron and steel. Everything collected was then to be taken to the designated auction house – this in the City of Scarlett, 115 kilometres Southeast of Benson. The contractors were also instructed to board up all civic buildings.

Benson, even in its tragic emptiness, retained a certain elegance. It became one of the iconic images of the times of climate crisis in the country. Photographers immersed themselves in finding ways to present its haunting voids. Their images appeared in numerous magazines and journals for several years. The state-gutted abandoned building designed by Andrew Jenson still asserted itself and commanded the gaze. But for all of its residual material presence, the city had disappeared, its life, energy, spirit and future all gone. One wonders, if the climate again changes, could it be reborn in perhaps two, three or four hundred years' time? Seeing the place is to entertain such wishful thinking. It looked like it was waiting.

HOURAGE

The impact of drought on crops, grass, trees and animals is simple and clearly evident: they die. The impact on people is also devastating, but unlike the environment, it is not always immediately visible. Drought kills many rural and remote cities. Their agriculture-dependent economy fails; those who can leave to find work elsewhere do so, inevitably businesses starting to close, and property values crashing. Hourage suffered this fate. Such observations have been made of many places in the world exposed to drought over eons.

Watching the world around you die is a harrowing experience. It has several psychological consequences. To make this clear, consider Laren's story.

For many generations, my family have been sheep farmers – sheep have been bred to produce fine wool. But that's now all over. We have had droughts in the past, never as bad as this current one. In common with many other farms in the area, we have suffered the same fate. Our entire world has come crashing down. Our entire flock was starving. The farm could not feed them, nor was there feed available to buy. Over a week, myself, my father, my two brothers shot 2,000 ewes and 300 rams. Then we piled them up with a front-end loader, poured petrol over them and watched them burn with tears in our eyes and pain in our hearts. The experience of what we had to do was obviously truly horrible, but the lasting inner reality was worse, especially for my father. What died for him was not just sheep but his world. He is now a different person. He eats very little, but drinks a lot, and does very little else. He is deeply depressed. For most of the day, he sits on the veranda and watches the breeze lift the dust of what once were lush pastures. We all have bad dreams. My mother cannot reach my father. Even when she tries to talk to him, he just says sorry and walks away. We worry he will commit suicide; many farmers have.

Kevin, my eldest brother, now has a job driving a water tanker for the Council. He does four daily runs taking water to farm households to keep them alive. Everyone tells the same story of despair. He is our only source of income. It keeps food on the table.

We are the lucky ones. For the moment, we still have a home. We don't have a big debt to pay off, as do many people who bought their farms in recent years, or borrowed to buy stock. On top of everything else, most of these people will lose their farms. Many have already filed for bankruptcy. In almost all cases, the banks are allowing people to stay on the farms until the market improves. At the moment, farms are unsellable, no matter what they farm. Apart from the three supermarkets, the two news agencies, the post office and the four banks – who have laid off staff and now only open three days a week – all other shops in the city are closed, as are many other businesses. The city is dying; no, it's dead. All the indications are that the heat will continue, the drought will not end, and within three or four years, the area will become uninhabitable. At the moment, this prospect is unspeakable in our household. My brothers and I know this to be certain. We will have to move south and look for work. Between the three of us, we do have some savings, not much, but enough to support the move. As far as I am concerned, I only have two choices: give up or make a new life. I'm not giving up. I'm looking for possibilities. What I do know is that I will never be able to work with animals again. The well of grief I fell into is too deep, the dreams I have are too vivid. As for our parents, we have no idea what they will do. It's impossible to even have the conversation. I did try to talk to my mother. I asked what she and Dad would do if there were no more rain? She looked at me for several minutes without saying anything, shrugged, and then said your father will think of something. She did not mean it and knew I did not believe her.

Fire

MOSSMAK

It was C48.5° and the asphalt on the road had melted to liquid. A young woman on a small motorcycle came around the bend at a moderate speed, and the machine slid from under her. She screamed as her arms and legs hit the very hot road. The whole one side of her body was black. A middle-aged man walking by ran to her aid and helped her to the footpath. While this was happening, a large four-wheel drive coming around the bend from the opposite direction hit and crushed the motorcycle, rupturing its fuel tank. The petrol, on reaching the machine's hot tailpipe, ignited. Within seconds the road was on fire. A fast-moving blue flame floated above it and travelled in both directions, lighting rising fumes from the asphalt. The once road was now a river of fire. The man and injured young woman had retreated from the path into a parking area in front of a car body shop, and two guys in overalls were carrying the woman inside, with the large man following behind them. By this time, the fire was now larger and spreading. Many roads were in flames. Parked cars were catching fire and exploding, timber power poles were alight and black smoke filled the air. Within two hours, scores of buildings were in flames, tinder-dry parks and gardens were burning. The wind was now carrying burning embers and cinders to untouched areas. Oxygen was being sucked out of the air and the fires were creating a climate of their own. Huge numbers of people fled. Many did not manage to – this transpired to be over 12 per cent of the population. No matter the size of the fire service, it would not have saved the city once the fire had taken hold.

By the following morning, some of the city was still burning, but mostly it was a smouldering expanse of gutted buildings, twisted and blackened metal, ash, bodies and emptiness. Some bodies were totally incinerated, some awaited collection and the process of identification – while the government would send in forensic identification teams, finding DNA samples to match would be extremely hard in many cases.

Late in the day, the first units of Army Engineers arrived. They had been assigned the task of making the city safe. Mostly, this meant demolishing structures that were dangerous and securing the city, now designated as a prohibited area. In the coming days, it would be visited by teams of investigators. It was still hot, and for most of the coming days, it would be over C40°, at least for another two weeks. Army medics were also there to assist. One detachment had been assigned to recover bodies. Not only was this a gruesome task, but searching for and extracting bodies from burnt and structurally unsound buildings was dangerous. The government had hired a fleet of refrigerated trucks to transport these bodies to an Air Force base, 40 kilometres away, where a temporary morgue was established. A large field hospital had also been set up on the base, together with a medevac transport capability. It would fly serious burn victims to hospitals with burn units around the country – the young woman whose accident started the fire being one of them.

A week after the fire, the government commissioned a federal inquiry. A year later, it issued its report. It concluded that it was not possible to eliminate risk from heat-produced solar radiation in an age of global warming. However, what was lacking in Mossmak was a simple and powerful warning system (audio and visual), as well as designated and clearly marked evacuation routes and a disaster contingency plan. The only places in the city that had a contingency plan were the two hospitals. Neither survived. Besides some of administrative, crisis-response and planning recommendations, its last major one was of particular interest. This was that Councils, nationally, be given the power to declare and enforce a state of 'urban arrest'. What this meant was that all traffic would stop and everyone on the street would seek indoor shelter. The point of this measure was to give emergency services immediate and unimpeded access to anywhere in the city in the fastest possible time.

Because the ashes of the dead were ingrained in the ruins, it was decided by the government not to rebuild all of the city. In these areas, existing structures would be demolished, all contaminated areas would be decontaminated and the land levelled. In times past, it could have been made into a forest, been given soil and seeded with native wildflowers. However, now these spaces would be paved, have a commemoration plaque, shade protection, water points and be designated as 'places of retreat'. The report also stated that a technical committee should be established within three months to examine increasing urban environmental risks and responses. (869).

SILL

The City of Sill has one of the biggest wood-chip-based paper-making plants in the world. Every week, several bulk carriers arrive at its port and discharge their cargo, which depending on the size of the ship, will be between 35,000 to 45,000 tonnes of chips. The port-side stockpile varies in size: it is rarely below 200,000 or over 250,000 tonnes. Making paper in plants in the city makes logistical sense. By eliminating almost all transport costs to plants elsewhere, a lot of money is saved.

. . .

It was C42° on the day of the fire. Spontaneous combustion is common in piles of green timber woodchips, especially if stored in warm or hot conditions. This is because heat is generated as organic material breaks down. If it isn't dissipated by good ventilation, the heat increases and eventually ignites. The management of such stockpiles is equipped to deal with such situations. But this day was different. The fire was deep in the pile, well established and went undetected. The fire conditions were the worst – it was a very hot day with a strong wind. The fire erupted and was immediately blasted by the wind. It soon became clear that the fire was not going to be able to be controlled. Hot ash and burning chips were soon blowing in the wind towards the city. There had been no rain for months. Trees and grass were igniting. Embers were landing in the gutters of houses, many filled with dried leaves that, in seconds, burst into flames. Roof timbers were quickly ignited. The same thing was happening when embers landed on the wooden decks of verandas of houses whose occupants were working or absent elsewhere. Soon, many houses in suburbs near the port were in flames. The bigger the critical mass of fire, the faster it spreads.

Soon warehouses, factories and commercial buildings were ablaze. The situation was out of control in a matter of an hour or so. Chaos ruled the streets. The traffic was logjammed, people were leaving their cars and fleeing in all directions, often the wrong ones. Looting of shops was starting to occur. As far as could be seen, the city had no contingency for such an event. There were no evacuation routes, and the fire department and police were totally overwhelmed. The speed at which order descended into complete disorder was extraordinary.

Sill General Hospital was on the southern edge of the city. Apart from a grass fire, with the help of the crew, a fire truck and hospital porters, there were extinguishers, so the hospital was spared. However, it was totally overwhelmed by the huge number of people suffering burns or injuries acquired while escaping from burning buildings or from motor accidents during manic road conditions. Even so, these people would have constituted only a small fraction of the population needing acute medical care.

It took eight days for all the fires to be extinguished. The city was a ruin. There were shells of a few buildings standing that might be repairable, but not many. Most were unstable and would have to be demolished. Ironically, the least affected area was the dockland. While the fire started there, the wind took it away within an hour. The wood-chip paper-making plant was totally destroyed. In all, over 80,000 people were rendered homeless. Some moved to relatives and friends in other cities; others, the old and frail, were taken to hotel or tented accommodation, while the majority were transported to two military camps to await the creation of temporary housing. A national clothing appeal was established, as was a financial aid programme, a psychological counselling service and a number of tent schools were set up, staffed by Sill teachers supported by the Department of Education. The economic scale of the disaster had thrown the insurance industry into turmoil.

The state government designated Sill as a major disaster area on day two. Emergency services from six other cities came to its aid. The federal government directed the Army Medical Corps to set up a field hospital, and burn units around the country activated plans to receive seriously burned patients. But all this took days, over which people died.

A Federal Commission of Inquiry was established with wide terms of reference. These included an examination of cause and legal liability, the economic and social impacts of the destruction of the city and the viability of the planning and reconstruction of a new city on the site of Sill or elsewhere. Doing all this was expected to take at least three years. Meanwhile, over 80,000-plus adults and children were facing the daily problem of dealing with the physical and mental loss of their homes, belongings, employment, income, and in many cases, the loss of friends and relatives.

CHENEN

The writer Fu Shen, many decades ago, documented the oppression of his nation's ethnic minorities, especially those who expressed dissent at their treatment by the government. The last article he wrote before he died, entitled 'Notes from the Underground', addressed what he called the 'silent insurgency'. He said it defined a group of radicals, of an unknown number who took direct action against the state, but never claimed ownership of it, and never claimed a name for themselves. Sometimes what they did was small, like putting sugar in the fuel tanks of government vehicles, or cutting power lines to government facilities. They also did more sophisticated and disruptive things, and they had some really smart hackers. One hacked into the annual financial reports of the income and investments of members of the ruling government. It showed that several of them had conflicts of interest that were being ignored. The result was that one Minister and two junior members of the government resigned. The outrage also forced the government to reform the reporting process and make it public.

Shen pointed out that such action was sporadic and had limited impact, but that it did result in the growth of a cadre of activists. As the reactionary government's policies increasingly disadvantaged the poor and marginal ethnic groups in the areas of employment, housing and education, many of the activists became more radical. The most radical formed a splinter group and created what they called a 'politics of fire' based on political arson. Their targets were selective, were not directed at people, and their destruction of property was predominantly symbolic. They waged 'war' on Airbnb and its reduction of available and affordable rental property (they hacked sites, poured oil in their trash cans and lit them, and torched one empty detached property.) On discriminatory employment policy (they picketed workplaces and set alight their placards before leaving), and on the cost of education, they exposed even 'free education' is not free, and money buys privilege (they organised student strikes and marches, plus burning school gates, fences and signs.) These actions were small, frequent, and widespread, and the political message was clear: set education free. They grew in number, divided communities and forced the government, while condemning 'mindless vandalism and extremism', to defend the lack of effective action: on housing; on racial discrimination; and also against the disabled. The poor job that the government was doing became visible like no other time before. As a result, public sentiment swung towards the activists. They recognised this and organised mass rallies outside government offices. Each time several hundred thousand people turned out. In the beginning, the police were only expecting a few thousand and were therefore unable to control the situation. Then the situation changed. At one rally among the crowds of thousands of angry people, there were a few who had come with concealed petrol bombs – they were not 'politics of fire' people.

First three people lit and threw the bombs against the office window of the Department of Defence; two hit their target, while one fell short. This action triggered dozens more people to do the same along the building's 120-metre frontage. Flames started to appear amidst the sound of alarms, as the crowd cheered. Police snatch squads tried to grab people, which led to fighting between crowd members and the police. Behind them, fire trucks were trying to reach the blaze. Using fire hoses to clear a path, it took them more than half an hour to reach the building. By this time, the crowd was breaking up and retreating. It was too late. The fire had taken total hold of the building; it could not be saved.

The city and the nation were completely shocked by the event. The staid and conservative image of the city was consumed by the fire. It was now a different place, one of frustration and anger. Nobody was killed, but the image of the city died, as did that of the government. The people went home, order was restored, nobody was arrested, a public inquiry was held, the government resigned, a new one was elected and the building was rebuilt. There was a clampdown on Airbnb, and new anti-discrimination laws were passed. But at a fundamental level, nothing changed, except for the image of the city.

Nurin

There are 12,000 tonnes of waste from the city of Nurin going into landfill every day. This equates to 4.38 million tonnes annually. The combination of moisture from leachates from waste and rain and the presence of around 10 per cent of oxygen can, and does, produce spontaneous combustion. The city had been dumping waste on its current landfill site for twenty-seven years. As a result, it was now spread over 820 square hectares, an area equal to around 200 football pitches.

Exactly where on the site spontaneous combustion started remains unclear, but once it did, it spread quickly. Such fires are hard to extinguish because they cannot be easily reached. Even when they appear to be extinguished, they go on smouldering. There have been such fires on the site before, but they either burnt themselves out or were controlled. This one was different. It really took hold and grew quickly. A huge volume of acrid smoke was produced that drifted over the city. The media passed on a directive from the Council that people should stay indoors and that all doors and windows should be closed. But many were on the street, working outdoors or travelling. Soon, people were presenting at hospital emergency rooms with respiratory problems, swollen and stinging eyes and there was an alarming number of heart attacks. Within two hours, the hospitals were struggling to cope. A full-scale medical emergency was announced. All medical staff were recalled to their workplace, stable patients without serious conditions were moved into corridors, non-critical cases on operating theatre lists were cancelled and the triage system was upgraded to code red.

Fighting the fire was really problematic. The impact was from the smoke, and bombing it with water made even more smoke as it lowered the rate of combustion. Higher combustion means less smoke. Using fire retardant is even more of a problem than water as it makes the smoke even more toxic, thus harmful for the eyes, skin and lungs. The city was in a double bind: it needed to put the fire out, but this would increase the impacts of the smoke. If it let it burn itself out, the impacts would be slightly lower but extend over a longer period of time. Either way, the city was being rendered dysfunctional and its economy was being seriously damaged. Many businesses were already on the edge. No cash flow for even one or two weeks would push them over the edge into bankruptcy. In the face of this situation, and on the advice of the Department of Health, together with information from the weather bureau, it was stated that the city should be evacuated until the fire is out. Apparently, infant mortality, and that of the aged, was increasing alarmingly. Acting on the basis of this information, the Council ordered the city should be evacuated and the fire extinguished as quickly as possible with all available means. At 11:20 a.m. on the same day, the decision was made to start the evacuation. The city's population of 1.2 million was to be moved by the state government.

The population was notified by all available media and instructed to drive to Air Force base Alpha 7 22 kilometres north on route 62. An evacuation centre was being established there by the Red Cross emergency command, with support from the Air Force. Aircraft hangars were being cleared, tents pitched and hygiene facilities established. Everyone was instructed to bring a blanket, pillow and their personal needs, including medication, for at least four days. The elderly and the sick would be housed in the aircraft hangars; a field hospital would be established, as would a field kitchen by the Army Catering Corps. The local police, with federal police support, equipped with protective clothing and breathing equipment, would be securing the city. The warnings broadcast by the media and police vehicles with loudspeakers stated that the evacuation was compulsory, that the city would not function and all services would be turned off. Anyone who stayed and was seen on the street would be arrested. Police patrols would be especially looking for people and signs of break-ins and looting. The messages given also emphasised the need for everyone to stay calm and act as instructed.

The medical officer said evacuating two hospitals at short notice to comparative medical facilities was impossible. She had made inquiries and established that it was possible to hire two very large industrial air scrubbers. These could be patched into the air conditioning systems of the respective hospitals. A skeleton staff would run them on a 'care on need basis'. Anyone who could be safely discharged would be by 6:00 p.m. and then taken to the Air Force base.

A pet sanctuary was being created at a large boarding kennel on a farm en route to the Air Force base. All pet owners had to drop their pets off at a collection point at the kennel en route to the base. Animal transport would be provided at the transport hubs. All cats and other small animals must be boxed, the boxes marked with the owner's name and address. All dogs must be registered on arrival at the booking tables at the base.

The overwhelming concern that preoccupied the Council was chaos and panic during the evacuation process. Next was putting the fire out quickly. The plan was to drop charges into the centre of the landfill site and then hit it with a massive amount of fire retardant. Once the fire no longer posed a problem, the mid- and long-term challenge was putting the city's economy back on its feet. On the one hand, there was the loss of working days and productivity and the possibility of a significant number of business closures. Then there were all the costs incurred by the fire and the evacuation, including cleaning up the city. There was a deposit of black soot on everything. Removal had to happen quickly and safely. The Council also real-ised that the trauma and disruption of evacuation would have had a big impact on very many people; they would need support. How the nation saw the city was another concern.

The whole evacuation process went as well as could be expected. There was a small amount of protest; these were a few scuffles, and twenty-eight people were arrested and held in custody on the Air Force base. There were a few vehicle breakdowns that posed minor problems, but prior contingent arrangements had been made with tow-trucks from outside the city to deal with this issue. Not unexpectedly most problems came from pet owners, some refusing to send them to the sanctuary. A few people hid and did not leave their homes. Tragically, this was not discovered until the population returned to the city. By this time, four of the fifty-one people who did this had died. All the animals taken to the sanctuary survived.

The fire was extinguished by the method indicated in three days. It took two months to clean the city. The economic impact was worse than expected. Likewise, the impact on the medical system was severe, and hospital waiting lists exploded. The city did disappear in a cloud of smoke for a while. When it reappeared, it was in mourning for its losses.

The experience, and the cost, diminished the health of the city's economy for several years. That such a big impact from what was first seen as a small recurrent problem – a fire in a landfill – was a sobering lesson.

ARILEKO

The Tashasi aluminium recycling factory was built on low-lying land on the outskirts of the City of Arileko in a newly created industrial complex. It produced two products: aluminium ingots and deoxidisers (a chemical agent that reduces the oxygen level in the steel-making process).

It had been raining for a week, and the Rinkin River had overflowed its banks and flooded land adjacent to the industrial complex. The water would reach it soon.

Permission to build in this part of the city indicated either incompetent planning or bribery, but equally, it marked a failure to undertake a risk assessment by building owners. On Friday afternoon, there was a storm and an exceptionally heavy dump of rain that dramatically worsened the situation. At 4:35, water reached the factory. The level rose quickly and penetrated an automated furnace pour. This caused a massive vapour explosion that took out half the side of the factory building. Molten metal flew in many directions, causing multiple fires. This included an adjacent plastic factory whose materials store was only ten metres from the once wall of the destroyed foundry. Fragments of this wall, together with molten metal, smashed through it and started a fire. The store contained many flammable chemicals.

The fire spread quickly. Within two hours, notwithstanding the arrival of firefighters, the fire had reached the company next to the raging inferno at RKM Plastics – the newly affected company was Zuma Tyres. With this factory alight, the situation got even worse. The whole area became enveloped in a cloud of black toxic smoke. The air was now a cocktail of toxic chemicals. The post-fire investigation identified them as cerebrogenic dioxin, hydrogen chloride gas, cyanide, carbon monoxide, sulphur dioxide, butadiene and styrene – all coming from the burning PVC, other plastics and rubber. Finally, the fire reached the Egal Furniture company, which, besides using timber and steel in its products, also use foam rubber, plastics and synthetic fabrics. Not only did this worsen the already bad situation, but it extended the area of air pollution well beyond the industrial area.

The large fire is very hard to fight. This one was attacked from the ground and the air. All the firefighters were wearing breathing apparatus; several were injured. Increasingly, smoke drifted across the city, leaving a grey greasy film on everything it touched. The smoke got into people's eyes, noses, mouths, lungs and bloodstream. TV, radio, social media and police speaker vans were telling everyone at home or work to shut all doors and windows and stay indoors until they were told the danger was over. There was a discussion by the Council on the viability of the evacuation of the city. However, the complexity and the time it would take to organise and do so, along with the exposure to the smoke during the process, would be too risky. How long it would take to extinguish the fire was unclear. There were arguments. A general call for assistance was made to the Department of Forests, which had four heavy-lift water bomber helicopters. There was also a request made for more breathing apparatus for hospitals, staff, police and ambulance services. People were already becoming sick, and the city hospital was in emergency mode. Health problems were going to extend into the future. The question of whose fault it was goes back to issues of due diligence, poor planning and a failure to identify and calculate risk.

As for the disappearance of Arileko, it was visible in its invisibility. Smoke covered everything. It turned out to be not simply a matter of washing the city down. What was deposited was corrosive as well as toxic. It required several decontamination exercises. The task would take many weeks, including the management of a huge amount of contaminated water and organic waste. Market gardens and domestic vegetable plots all had to be removed for safe disposal. Many animals were poisoned and had to be put down. People's lives were shortened. The public were angry; so were the media. Who to blame, who is liable? Who will pay? The one thing that was clear, these issues were going to take a lot of litigation and time to resolve.

DISAPPEARANCE
BY THE PURELY UNNATURAL • 3

While there is a history of the disappearance of cities by natural means, almost as long as the existence of cities themselves, our species' actions have significantly added to this history. Human beings collectively also have a history of destroying cities, by means of their own invention. War, with its missiles, bombs and shelling, and before this, fire, is the most obvious example. Industries (and industrial accidents) have also directly destroyed cities. The ability to destroy by unnatural means has escalated over time and continues to do so.

War and Other Conflicts

HERRESTA

Joseph had lived his entire life in the small rural city of Herresta. There was nothing in any way remarkable about the old man. Today he did what he did every day since his retirement. He woke at dawn and said good morning to the small framed photograph of Mary, his deceased wife, that sat on the small table beside his bed. After spending ten minutes in the bathroom, it was always ten minutes, he made a pot of coffee. Putting a small notebook and pencil in his pocket, he took the pot and a cup to the veranda, placed them on one end of the wooden bench he had made over fifty years ago, and sat down. After drinking the first cup, as always, he listed the tasks for the day. He worked for two hours before breakfast and then two more hours after it. That was his working day every day, no matter the weather, and there was always something to do in the greenhouse if it was bad.

Today he pricked out lettuce seedlings and prepared the garden bed where he would plant them once they had grown to a size to survive. The next job on his list was to prune the lower stems on newly established tomato plants; this to force growth to the fruit rather than to the leaves. Once finished, he turned the sprinkler on to give everything a drink before the day became warm. After twelve minutes, he turned it off and headed to the kitchen to make breakfast and listen to the morning news. It started, as it had for the past four months, with news of the war – the border war 350 kilometres away. It was not a big war; they flared up every few years. They caused problems for cities nearer to the border, but up until now, not Herresta.

Joseph poured milk, then honey, on the same brand of cereal he had eaten for at least twenty years. Once finished, he would make more coffee and toast two slices of bread. Getting up to fill the kettle, he heard the sound of an aircraft. They were low, loud, getting louder and were nearing the city. He put the kettle on the stove and went out into the garden to see them [...]

Yarwui

This is a story that is not unique, but one that is now sadly being repeated in many places around the world in recent times.

The event that triggered what was to become a major urban disaster started on the first day after the new year. It was a riot of epic proportion. The reason for this was not hard to discern. Hundreds of thousands of people living in Heno, the informal section of the city, crossed the bridge over the river dividing the poor from the rich and invaded the downtown area. The more their circumstances worsened, the angrier and more aggressive the Heno community became. Three issues converged to shift their anger into action. The first was the displacement of their domestic labour force by robots; the second was the banning of Heno recyclers. They travelled the entire city with their colourful carts, picking cans, bottles and other recyclables from trash cans and skips. Wealthy suburbanites hated them. They said they stole, were an undesirable 'blight on the streets', and their presence even 'lowered the value of their property'. On both counts, these actions made the already poor poorer. Added to these two issues was the conduct of the police, who harassed them and who were empowered to 'stop and search' at will. Their claim was that the poor only came downtown to beg and steal. Recently, the police became more forceful in excluding Heno people from downtown, especially in the evenings and at weekends. The violence and abuse in the way that did this became another flashpoint for action.

On New Year's Eve, the police placed barriers across the north and south bridges and turned all Heno people back when they tried to enter the downtown area. The next day, the day of the riot, was a public holiday. The police had kept the barriers in place and were there in force. A large crowd at the north bridge rushed the barriers, pushed them over and stormed the police. Overwhelmed, the police retreated. Over the next few hours, tens of thousands of Heno men, women and children flooded into downtown. The police had no ability to hold this mass of people in check. Disorder now displaced repressive order, but at what cost and with what consequences? It did not take long for this question to be answered.

Within a matter of minutes of the first wave of people filling the streets of downtown, cars were overturned and spilled fuel was set alight, shop windows were smashed and stores were looted. The blossoming of chaos happened in an instant. Any resistance by the police was smothered by the sheer scale of an unstoppable tsunami of bodies. Anyone in its path was knocked over and trampled. The air was quickly filled with smoke, the ground littered with broken glass, abandoned spoils by looters and bloodied bodies. The mass continued forward, leaving an appalling detritus in its wake.

While all this was happening downtown, another mass of people, maybe 20,000 to 30,000 people, had crossed the southern bridge. This took them into the industrial area. They were met by a small number of security personnel and a larger cohort of police who had been mobilised to meet them. As it was a holiday, the place was empty. There had only been a short amount of time for the police to organise their resistance. Fire hoses had been run out and connected to hydrants; as soon as people appeared, they were turned on. Then there was one line of police in riot gear, armed with long batons, carrying shields and wearing gas masks, and behind them, another line, all armed with riot guns able to shoot rubber projectiles or tear-gas grenades. Behind them were police vehicles blocking the road and even more police. When the mass was within about 100 metres of the police line, about a dozen officers with rifles appeared in front of those in riot gear. They were ordered to fire and shot a volley

into the air. At this, the mass fragmented. Some ran behind industrial buildings, others jumped down onto the path running along the
river bank. Within a minute, the police were facing an empty road.
Meanwhile, the dispersed rioters were getting into factory yards,
where they found discarded wooden pallets and scrap metal, trucks
and vans, waste bins filled with cans and bottles. In minutes, they
were armed with lengths of wood, spades, chains, metal rods, plus
hammers and wrenches taken from tool boxes on trucks. They also
managed to pierce fuel tanks, find rags in trucks and were making
petrol bombs from the bottles in the bins. Once armed, they split
into groups, scattering in various directions.

While all this was happening, the police and the security personnel had reorganised into several groups, and a police helicopter was
in the air. At most, they were 400, and all they could do was defend
property as directed from the air. They were completely unable to
control the situation and had no chance of getting reinforcements.

The rioters managed to cause chaos. Petrol bombs were used
mostly to start fires. The warehouse of an office furniture company,
and one full of beds and mattresses, were two of many buildings set
ablaze. Large numbers of vehicles were torched, including twelve
trucks in a transport yard. The fires spread, and the industrial area
turned into one of low-level urban warfare, with the police eventually
shooting to kill. Scores of rioters died, and even more were wounded.
Eleven policemen, four policewomen and two security guards were
also killed, and around fifty were wounded. After two and a half
hours, large numbers of rioters headed across fields towards the
southern suburbs of the city. Others, with their walking wounded,
returned home. The police, their numbers depleted, and with all
their vehicles damaged, did not pursue. They stayed and, with little
success, fought fires. The helicopter stayed in the air and followed the
rioters, but it had no resources to direct.

By this time the government had declared a state of emergency and directed the army to the city to restore order; several thousand troops arrived by mid-afternoon. By this time the rioters had spread out across the suburbs – most of their populations having fled. The rioters went from street to street breaking into homes and setting them alight.

It took the army and the police four days to stabilise the situation. Almost all fires burnt themselves out; their scale and number were obviously well beyond the means of the fire department. The event shocked the nation and the world. Over 1,500 citizens died, more than 12,000 were injured, 149 policemen and women lost their lives and over 2,000 rioters died. The number of the injured is not known, but was estimated to be of the order of 20,000. The population of Heno was more than 700,000 impoverished souls.

Events at Yarwui that day of shame struck fear into many hundreds of cities globally, which were equally divided between the well-off formal areas and those that were informal and populated by the poor. As the leaders and populations of these cities worldwide knew, what happened in Yarwui could happen in their city at any time.

Yarwui no longer existed as it was. As a viable city, it had disappeared. What remained was a shell of its former self. Its material fabric, including many thousands of homes, was burnt and trashed. Its economy was ruined, from the loss of goods, business, as well as the cost of damage. The repair and remaking of the city would take years. But who would want to invest or live in the city? Those people who could leave had left. The people of Heno were now not only more impoverished but seen as the absolute enemy – for months the streets were patrolled by troops in armoured personnel carriers. Despair defined the state of mind of the entire population of the 2.4 million, be they rich or poor, who still lived in Yarwui. Many of the people who took flight never came back, not even to collect their belongings. Many of the businesses that burnt out never reopened. No business, home or vehicle in the city was able to be insured at a price that any but the richest could afford. The name of the city remained, as did roads, infrastructure and buildings, but the city as a mixed society, culture and economy did not survive. It was an empty shell. Everyone knew it had no future. Rebuilding would never be total; the repair of the social fabric of the city would not be possible, and its economy would decline, with people and businesses continuing to move elsewhere whenever they could. The people of Heno, now totally ghettoised, faced an even starker unfolding choice: stay and perhaps starve, or move and become homeless.

Juria

By any measure, the insurgency was a small war. At most, 2,000 badly armed insurgents faced an army of 58,000 well-trained, well-armed troops. The insurgents had no intention of directly engaging them. They did not delude themselves; they did not expect to win. What they were fighting for was to do enough economic damage to get into a position of negotiation, to improve the conditions and treatment of the marginalised people they believed they represented. Their struggle started in the City of Juria.

It was from there that they launched eight kamikaze drones with explosive warheads against four 200-tonne hydrogen tanks at the major plant of Nathydro – the nation's main producer of hydrogen. They knew that as soon as a tank was hit and the hydrogen was exposed to air, it would explode. This happened, and the explosion was massive. Burning debris ignited many other installations in the industrial park. It took all the resources of the fire department eighteen hours to bring the fire under control. An estimated 800 million dollars of damage was done. Besides the loss of the hydrogen plant, four other businesses were destroyed and 800-plus jobs were lost. There was an economic chain reaction. Many small and medium-sized suppliers to the large businesses failed and went out of business, and a few survived, but scores of jobs were lost.

Not only was the impact on the local economy large, but the shortage of hydrogen brought transport and bus companies with vehicles running on it to a halt. Likewise, one of the city's main electricity substations was destroyed in the fire. This meant 40 per cent of the city was without power for a week, and then only with a restricted supply. The economic impact on the nation was significant, and on the city severe. Then the insurgents struck again. This time, a smaller drone struck a large natural gas storage and distribution plant on the edge of the city. Again, a big fire. This resulted in a large number of businesses dependent on natural gas – like bakeries and caterers – being closed until they could be resupplied, but this would be only on a rationed basis. Tens of thousands of domestic users of gas for cooking and heating, in and beyond the city, faced an even worse situation. Some waited for several weeks without gas to be supplied from an alternative supplier. The government, which ruled with a slim majority before this crisis, now looked very insecure. Industry and the public demanded action. The insurgents calculated that one more action would bring the government down. The government, knowing it was in danger of losing power, declared a state of emergency and martial law. It also called up the army reserve, imposed a curfew and took command of essential services.

The insurgents changed tactics. Rather than make another strike against an economic target, they struck the main police station in Juria with three drones. Nobody was killed; there were three minor injuries, two from broken glass and one from a roof tile hitting patrol car crews in the car park. Two days later, a car bomb exploded outside the mayor's office as he was leaving at the end of the day, killing him. A week later, five fast-food outlets were firebombed and burnt out during the night when they were closed. One was in Juria; the others in two other cities. Effectively, this was psychological warfare. The combination of troops on the streets of Juria and the attacks pushed some people, already afraid and unsettled, over the edge. They moved out. A significant number in the city were on the verge of panic. The insurgents knew this. They struck two petrol stations in Juria, causing fires that destroyed nine cars, a truck and three shops. Seventeen people were injured. Many people in the suburbs stayed home. Around 15 per cent of the inner city moved to friends or relatives in the suburbs or left town, these were young people without ties. Most people went to work, only shopped for essentials and nobody went out in the evening. Within a few weeks, small businesses, especially cafes, fast-food restaurants (which also found it hard to get delivery drivers), nightclubs, cinemas and bars started to close. People started presenting to doctors with depression.

The government announced that it would not negotiate with insurgents and terrorists, but in private it engaged a human rights lawyer to act as a mediator to identify their demands and to explore conditions for a meeting in consultation with the prime minister and the ministers of home affairs and defence.

The demands of the insurgents were for their people to be recognised within the Constitution with a treaty that defines their rights and status as first nation people, gives reparation for their displacement from their traditional lands and makes restitution for the violent treatment and suffering imposed upon them by colonial powers and subsequent ruling regimes. As the mediator knew, the government was not going to capitulate to these demands. She also knew what they would do – string them along, buy time and hope the resistance would weaken. It didn't. Compromise and gesturalism had a short life. Decline set in. Strategically, the insurgents became more vocal. They made their case, became more political, with a campaign against military recruitment, with occasional soft strikes against military targets, especially unattended aircraft using crawler drones at night (defence against airborne drones having become much improved) to let the government know they could still be, and become, more dangerous. This was the future, one of national insecurity.

Juria remained a city in decline. Few of the people who left returned, and the economy did not 'bounce back'. Investors shied away, and the population aged. What it once was gone, what remained was a city with a past and a diminishing future.

CONNORVILLE AEROTROPOLIS

At the time of its construction, Connorville Aerotropolis was the largest on the planet and one of the newest and most important centres of advanced defence industry development. It had two especially high-profile manufacturers: Sparta Air Defence Systems and Ronstrom laser ship protection technology. There were also substantial industry clusters in the areas of medical and nanotechnologies. Six major airlines operated out of the airport: two airfreights, four passengers.

The mood of the Aerotropolis distinctly changed when the clouds of war darkened. The political view was that conflict was likely to break out before the end of the year. The most discernible marker of concern and the mood of change was the arrival of two of the army's air defence missile batteries. This communicated to everyone, if they did not already know, that the Aerotropolis was deemed to be a significant target. Reactions ranged from mild concern to outright fear. What really shifted the bias of concern to fear was when a surveillance drone was spotted and shot down with a TDCD (tactical drone counter drone). The TV news crew who were waiting to cover the arrival of the Minister for Trade and Industry, who was flying in to open a new nanomedical research centre at the Aerotropolis created by NKV Medical and the National University, captured the strike. They obtained images of the whole incident, and it was broadcast on the 6:00 p.m. news nationwide. The Ministry of Defence was asked to comment on the identity of the downed drone, to which they replied that it was still under investigation.

Up until the arrival of the air defence missile batteries and the downing of the drone, most of the public's concern about the Aerotropolis had been about aircraft noise, especially at night – it operated twenty-four-seven, heavy laden big cargo planes made a lot of noise. The now 20,000-plus people living at the Aerotropolis joined forces with the wider public concern about living in the target zone of an adversary. The projected glittering star of the place of a techno-logical wonderland was appearing to be tarnished. Perceptions of the Aerotropolis changed. Now seen as a target, shares crashed, people left and those businesses that could move without major economic and organisational trauma moved.

YELLOW HILL

Situated in the most remote corner of the northern heathland, the Yellow Hill biological warfare research centre faded into its landscape almost unnoticed. Once fully operational, with a staff of eighteen scientists, four administrators and a rotating six-person security detail, it was now only a storage facility for its deadly past productive output. It ceased having a research function over a decade ago, but security had to continue 24/7. The condition and safety of everything stored had to be checked and maintained. It was now staffed by two security officers and two technical officers who controlled the facility's high-security entrance and its bank of security cameras. Any security breach automatically triggered a response from a SWAT-type reaction team. The storage area was managed by two technical officers. The security and technical officers both rotated with two other corresponding grades of officers on a ten-days-on, four-days-off rota.

All of the deadly material amassed over time was held on shelves in rooms with airlocks in a bomb-proof bunker deep under the building.

• • •

The Ministry Board of Inquiry established that Yellow Hill was the source of the Smallpox Variola virus, which caused a national crisis. They found that technical officer George Kenton had infected himself, then waited eleven days until a mild fever became apparent – meaning he was now infecting others. He then drove for five hours to the national capital, parked his car in a parking garage near his destination, the Central Railways station. Once there, he mixed with as many people as possible, including time spent in a crowded, stuffy, poorly ventilated waiting room. He also visited two restaurants and a newsagent-cum-bookstore. His aim was to infect as many people as he could – this in the knowledge that the people he infected would travel to many parts of the country as carriers of the virus.

After two hours at the station, Kenton returned to his car and set in the direction of his home south of Yellow Hill. Forty minutes outside the city, he left the freeway and joined a two-lane country road. He then drove for about five minutes before accelerating to a high speed and crashing into a large tree. The car was a total wreck. It was not possible to tell if the action was an accident, because he was unwell and unable to see properly, or if it was a deliberate act to end his own life. For this reason, the coroner removed ambiguity and recorded the cause of death as 'massive brain injury' caused by the impact of the accident. Although wearing rubber gloves, one of the first responders to the scene of the crash became infected and died.

As a result of his actions, tens of thousands of people became infected with smallpox. Very many of them died. Kenton had achieved his aim.

For decades, smallpox was regarded as having been eradicated. It was celebrated as the most successful of all vaccination programmes. Although stored at Yellow Hill as a biological weapon, its value as such was long gone, as so many people would be immune. However, because of the rise of the anti-vaxxer movement, there were now a significant number of people in the population unvaccinated by intent or by parental default, Kenton being one of them. Of all the people he came into contact with, it was these who were the ones that died. As the Board of Inquiry made clear, the impact of his actions went well beyond the cause of death. While the numbers were much lower than the Covid-19 pandemic of many years ago, it had a much higher survival rate. An estimated 12 per cent of the population were unvaccinated. There were many who did not know if they had been vaccinated or not.

So, there were lockdowns, school closures, people forced to work at home, businesses forced to close – some never reopening. The emergency laws imposed were strictly enforced. The economy took a big hit. Smallpox generated a high level of fear and the anxiety this generated meant that there was a great deal of stress and mental illness. Unsurprisingly, the medical service came under an enormous amount of pressure: getting a large amount of smallpox vaccine and injecting large numbers of people was a big challenge, as was managing contagion. Huge amounts of personal protective equipment had to be purchased, as did disinfectant – anything that anyone with smallpox came into contact with had to be disinfected. As always, misinformation has become an omnipresent problem.

With a highly contagious disease like smallpox – transmitted by bodily contact, by air and from touching infected surfaces – present in a city, it disappears as itself and becomes an alien environment. It becomes a place of recoil, a background of danger. The forces that animate everyday urban life largely cease to function. Workplaces, bars, cafes, restaurants, clubs, cinemas, theatres, gyms, sports venues, shops, buses and trains are all becoming empty.

The Board of Inquiry spent much time trying to discern Kenton's motive. They found nothing in his background. He was a single man, 38 years of age. He had never been in trouble and had no history of being politically active. His parents had separated; his father was dead, his mother had remarried and lived overseas and he had a younger brother serving in the Air Force. People interviewed during the inquiry all said the same thing – that he was quiet, unassuming;

some said boring. He neither drank nor smoked. His main hobby was photography, and he was also keen on fly fishing. Without evidence, the most likely motive for his action was thought to be an attempt to eliminate the anti-vaxxers. They came into the view as an issue after two interviews with his technical officer colleague and a friend. They told the inquiry that he had expressed his dislike and even contempt for anti-vaxxers on several occasions.

Buit

This city was wiped off the face of the Earth without the slightest damage. Its destruction confirmed a fear that had existed around the world for many decades.

The day was warm, the sky was blue. The hijacked Grumman Agcat crop sprayer came out of the west, flying slow and low at midday. It started to discharge its tanks, charged with water and 4 kilograms of anthrax spores. Multiple runs over the entire city infected tens of thousands of people immediately as they inhaled spores in the air. All of them were dead within a few days. Those who came into contact with contaminated surfaces also became sick, but they could be treated. But the numbers completely swamped the medical system, and many of them died. Within a week, over a third of the city's 1.1 million residents were dead. Its workforce was massively depleted, and with everyone confined to their homes, the city began a massive decontamination at the government's direction, by the Army Corps of Engineers. The city ceased to function, much of its infrastructure paralysed, and the city water supply was contaminated. No public transport was able to run, hospitals were overwhelmed and operating with less than half their staff; the same was true of the police and fire services.

All this, and more, was down to two terrorists whose plane was abandoned in a field next to the freeway 12 kilometres outside of the city. Who they were, their organisation, if any, and why Buit: their overarching motive for the attack was never established.

The economic impact on the city was massive. Without a viable workforce, businesses collapsed, many thousands of working days were lost and the cost of cleaning up the city and returning it to function took a year. The impact on people's lives was enormous. The psychological impact was such that it would last a lifetime. People had breakdowns, depression was rife, huge numbers of people suffered from post-traumatic stress, and there were hundreds of suicides. Materially, the city looked the same, but it was transformed into another reality dominated by fear and depression. Visitors kept away; the city acquired a stigma, and the food and entertainment culture of the city dwindled to almost nothing. The social life of the city also died – friends and family grew apart. From the scores of hotels, only five stayed in business. Filling job vacancies was really hard; it was not a city that people wanted to move to or live in.

Without question the city as it was known had disappeared.

MARRETTE

Urban warfare obviously destroys the city, partially or totally. We have all seen images of cities reduced to rubble by artillery and tank shells, bombs, missiles and drones – some experiencing such horrors. Marrette is one of those cities, but people still fight in and over the rubble. By intent or default, hospitals, schools, churches, aged care homes, domestic tower blocks, as well as factories, offices and individual homes become targets if deemed to be strategic or harbouring an adversary and are levelled. To call civilians collateral damage is to misrepresent; in truth they are either direct targets or deemed to be expedient. There is no morality, justice, compassion or humanity in urban warfare; it's either kill or be killed.

Refi is seventeen. He has been fighting for two years. His father was killed a year ago, and his brother is alive but lost both legs, blown off by a mortar shell. He does not know where his mother is. His only ambition is to stay alive. This is the only reason he fights. Kill or be killed is his mantra. He does not think about his future. The future is tomorrow. His base in the black tower 51 is also his home. He is in the combat group Tango Seven. Nothing is certain; damage is constant. Refi eats and sleeps when he can, fights when he is told to, or when attacked. He has nowhere else to go. It has been like this every day for seven months. His people are not winning, but neither are they losing. He has no idea how long the fighting will continue. The reason for the war was to save the country from invaders; now it's just to survive. The message from the commander is always the same: 'Stay strong, hold your ground, attack when you can, time is with us.'

If you ask Refi what he wants, he will tell you that he wants the war to be over. He wants a home to go to. He wants good food. He wants to sleep as long as he likes. He says he can't think beyond these things. He wants more out of life, but he cannot imagine what this more might be. What he knows with absolute certainty is that to keep his life he has to take the life of another. There is no outside to the inside of the death-world in which Refi dwells. He is too tired to dream; he is glad of this as he knows what he would dream about.

Louiserae

With remarkable finesse, Louiserae managed to combine all the shortcomings of modernist urban planning in one place. They sliced the city with multi-lane highways, created windswept public housing estates of tower blocks, lacking social and retail facilities, that within a decade had dysfunctional elevators, urine-smelling floor wells and tags denoting different drug dealer territories.

Nobody lived in the city centre. It was a no-go zone after 8:00 p.m., due to the clashes between competing ethnic and all-white far-right gangs, and the violent response of SWAT teams. Rising temperatures, increased by vehicle exhaust, meant the thermal mass of this 'concrete jungle' never cooled and made it unbearable. In every way, it was a nasty place, a reality confirmed by the city's homicide and domestic violence record. The bad situation was made worse by the way the media sensationalised it.

A combined study by the State Departments of Planning, Housing and Social Justice concluded that 40 per cent of the city should be levelled and rebuilt as medium density, along with social amenities (pre-school centre, park, public toilets, small retail complex and a bus terminal). This was about the same percentage of the city's medium density housing that had been demolished and replaced by the tower blocks. It was not in good condition, although it could have been refurbished for a fraction of the cost of constructing the blocks.

Around half of the public housing population would be relocated to the new developments of the city. Who would stay and who would move created a lot of friction. The expectation was that good Council tenants would be selected and offered the opportunity to move, while those with a poor record of property damage and rent default would not. The media inflamed this prospect, but the Council asserted it was incorrect. Nobody believed them. The social division within the city became exposed and raw.

The trouble started with a few protest marches, resulting in some broken windows and minor altercations between protesters and police. Then the police adopted a harder line and arrested thirty protesters trying to enter the Council office building. Within a few weeks, police cars and police stations were being petrol bombed. The area became a magnet attracting protesters from across the city. Then, different factions of the social divide clashed. Shops were damaged, there was looting, people were injured and more people were arrested. It was a bad situation, but there had been many much worse around the world in previous decades. However, the damage done to Louiserae was deep and long-term. Businesses that could move elsewhere did, as did people with money. The unemployment level increased from 4.6 per cent to 14.8 per cent in just eight weeks. The rateable base of the city dramatically dropped, as did the city's ability to attract investment and raise money.

Louiserae no doubt would stagger on without its redevelopment, and with some help from the state, yet with an expectation of continuous decline. Its population was insecure, old antagonisms remained and new ones arrived. The number of people suffering from mental illness was alarming. While still standing, the city had effectively destroyed itself and unless some unknown force arrived to revitalise it, it would disappear in every respect except its abandoned buildings.

MINONETA

The city was over 1000 kilometres from the war zone, but was deeply impacted by what was happening there. This was true of many other cities, towns and villages in the region.

The war had been going on for over a year. It was not going well by any measure based on the value of life. Tactical nuclear weapons were being used. Every nation on the planet was worried. There were fears that the situation could escalate to a full-scale nuclear conflict. It was spring, and the winds at this time of the year tended to be westerly. The thing that the people of Minoneta were frightened of, in common with people everywhere, was radiation. Government warnings and instructions just added to the general level of anxiety. People mostly took three kinds of action. They partied like crazy, took off to somewhere else they believed to be safe or started to board up their home, plug every possible hole or tape cracks that might allow air into indoor spaces. They bought and hoarded vast quantities of dried and canned food, as well as cartons of bottled water. An impending sense of panic was palpable.

The city came to a grinding halt. People stopped going to work, but pubs were packed. At home or in the pubs, people were glued to the TV screen. Every observed event of the war was reported and scrutinised in great detail by informed and ill-informed pundits alike.

At 7:00 a.m. on a cool Monday morning in October, a 100-kiloton nuclear bomb was dropped on a still sleepy Minoneta. The blast was equivalent to 1,000 tons of TNT. The whole centre of the city was flattened, and surrounding blast damage was extensive. Radiation from such a bomb decays quickly – people knew this. The government had already mailed instructions to all cities in the nation. The few radio and TV media outlets still broadcasting repeated the instructions on the hour, all day every day.

All inhabitants of the affected city stayed in their homes, with all windows and doors closed, for a minimum of four weeks. These surviving residents of the city were paralysed between two kinds of fear: of being affected by the bomb that had dropped, and the fear of another one arriving. A week after the blast, the casualty figures were published – 24,786 people died and 42,321 were injured, 13,346 seriously. The use of the bomb was an attempt to end the war by terror. It did not succeed. The war continues.

Within six weeks, people, in numbers, were back on the streets that still existed. The level of fear stayed high. Almost all families with children sent them to friends or family outside the city, or left it completely. Besides making damaged buildings safe, no work on the city has been done. Its fate was bound to the outcome of the war, which was not going to be good. The mood of the people was dark. They knew the heart of their city had been destroyed literally and in spirit, and that their future was disappearing.

ERON

Everyone knew Eron as an edgy border city. Like all such cities, it was a place of shady deals, drugs, vice and violence. But it had character; it was not boring and so attracted an amalgam of interesting people – writers, artists, musicians, political radicals, plus the bad and the mad.

The reactionary right-wing general who ruled the bordering nation was partly elected on an anti-immigration ticket. He came to power on the promise that he would round up and deport all 'illegals' in the country, and do it within the first sixty days of coming to office. With disregard for even the most basic human rights, he set out to do this with brute force. Within thirty days, he had over 7,000 'illegals' rounded up and imprisoned in detention centres. The first batch was taken in ten buses to Eron and then to the border. After being processed, they passed into the no-man's land between the two immigration facilities. They clearly could not go back to where they had just been deported, and it looked like they were unable to go forward and return to their homeland. There was a lot of shouting and screaming. They were in limbo for several hours until four army trucks and a group of soldiers arrived and took them away. Presumably, they were headed for another detention centre.

Five days later, a second group of buses arrived at Eron with another 500 deportees heading for the border. Just as the first bus approached a set of lights on the edge of downtown, a young guy in an old battered Toyota Hilux drove towards the first bus from the opposite direction, with a girl in the back throwing spikes made of welded large bent nails in front of the buses. As the first bus screeched to a halt, the one behind it shunted into its back. Each bus carried fifty deportees and five armed guards. Like the first batch, each deportee had their wrists cuffed with plastic ties.

As soon as the buses stopped, the doors opened and two guards jumped out, weapons wereready. It was a rehearsed drill. They were met with a hail of fire from a dozen or so shooters firing assault rifles from behind parked cars. It was a planned ambush. Once all the guards were downed, the shooters ran forward. At the same time, the 'illegals' were streaming off the buses. As soon as they met the shooters, their ties were cut, and they scattered in multiple directions. Fearing for their lives, the bus drivers also took off. Within minutes, the local police and many ambulances arrived to greet the carnage. Of the fifty guards shot, two were still alive, but not long enough to make it to the hospital. If any attempt was made to recapture the 'illegals', it was token and unsuccessful. They were in friendly territory. Within a few hours, federal investigators arrived by helicopter with a forensics team. By that time, all bodies were in the local morgue and the local police had secured the very large crime scene. The feds were there for three days documenting everything, taking samples, interviewing witnesses and the bus drivers, who returned to the buses, all of which had been damaged by gunfire, but not immobilised.

The media coverage of the attack shocked the nation and projected Eron into the national spotlight. It also shocked what was an almost unshockable city. Within just a few weeks, the city returned to its state of relative obscurity. This is how the population liked it – it was a city that traded concealment and disappearance rather than revelation and notoriety.

The search for the escapees, while completely unsuccessful, angered many already pissed-off people. In the city who had their property searched and who were questioned by federal investigators. The attack did not stop the deportation process.

The report published after the inquiry into the Eron bus attack was critical of the convoy not being well protected. It said it also evidenced a security intelligence failure. The immediate effect was to affirm that the process should continue, but that transportation should be militarised. This meant that the buses were accompanied by an armoured escort, with one acting 'as point' going ahead to check for anything of concern on the route. In addition, the route taken would be changed with each journey.

FIRTELL

Amtex CM was the largest producer of hydrogen cyanide in the country: its output exceeded 140 metric tons per day. At any one time, the plant could hold between 10,000 and 12,000 metric tons in tank storage. Hydrogen cyanide is also called prussic acid. It is widely used in the production of synthetic fibres, plastics, dyes and pesticides. It is also used in fumigation, electroplating and mining, and to synthesise other chemicals. As a liquid, it is pale blue; as a gas it is clear. As a chemical asphyxiant, it interacts with oxygen in the body, especially in the brain, heart and lungs – exposure to it can be fatal.

. . .

The war started in the early spring. By summer, the fighting had spread to the border region. Both sides constantly fought for air superiority, but neither fully gained it. Towards the end of summer, an event occurred that changed the course of the war. The Amtex CM plant was hit by a cruise missile. It not only ruptured multiple hydrogen cyanide storage tanks but also started a fire in an adjacent plastics factory. The result was that a huge cloud of gas formed and enveloped a large part of Firtell, a city of over 500,000 people. More than half the population died within thirty-six hours. Most of the remaining were seriously ill. The action was designated as being against the civilian population. It had no strategic military value and was thus was deemed to be an act of terror and a war crime. It was condemned by the international community. The leaders of the offending nation's four neighbouring countries met and demanded a ceasefire, saying if this did not happen, they would form a coalition and join forces with the aggrieved nation. The ceasefire occurred, and soon after, the war ended. The attack on the plant was referred to the International Court of Justice.

The contaminated city, with its depleted and damaged population, was the latest international symbol of the madness of late-modern industrial warfare. The government demanded reparation. As ever, the wheels of justice slowly turned. The same was not true for biology. Hydrogen cyanide exposure can have long-term and serious effects on the body, including on the brain, the central nervous system and the heart, as well as producing changes in mood and personality. Likewise, it contaminates organic matter in the environment. Therefore, there were also major issues of 'the disposal' of dead people, animals, plant matter and the management of more than 200,000 survivors. They needed immediate and likely long-term treatment. They were distributed in hospitals across the country – putting massive pressure on the nation's medical system. And then what to do about the city? In so many ways, without a single building being damaged, the city had been destroyed socio-culturally and economically. It could not be easily decontaminated: hydrogen cyanide lingers, stays in enclosed spaces and remains a danger. All clothing and fabrics contaminated by hydrogen cyanide have to be bagged and sealed, or boxed, in biohazard containers. Conducting this action for an entire city is a massive exercise.

Survivors were distributed among twelve hospitals around the country. The city was empty and entry was prohibited. Its outer perimeter was patrolled by a specially created federal police unit on the ground and in the air by helicopters. If the surviving population returned, they would be unevenly spread across a dysfunctional city. The staff losses mean that the operational structure of the city cannot be made to function. Bringing the material and social infrastructure back into service, rebooting the economy, reconstructing public services and the system of administration in a city of disconnected fragments would be extremely hard. But nothing happens until the decontamination process is completed. Added to all this are the massive legal problems with the ownership of the property, businesses and funds of the dead – just getting the needed information is a major problem. Essentially, people cannot return unless the city becomes functional. But for the city to become functional, people have to return. All this requires the creation of an organisational structure.

In the face of all these problems, a study to review action options was conducted. The process took six months; it put a plan to the national and state governments that they jointly create a Firtell reconstruction commission to oversee:

- A temporary housing programme for the displaced population;
- An interim legal and administrative body to deal with and oversee the reconstruction process;
- A planning process to select an area, or areas, of the city for a population of 220,000 people;
- An economic development unit to assist businesses in a position to re-establish themselves in the city;
- The development of new business opportunities;
- The scoping of a contamination, retrofit and infill programme for the selected areas; a 'mothball' area for an additional 50,000 people from standing building stock; and a demolition and remediation programme for the remainder of the city, with a material recovery programme and the establishment of a regional material reuse centre – all works subject to tender.

The plan was accepted, funding and investment partner relations were established and work began. It took six years to complete, but the remodelled Fertell Nova started being repopulated after two years. Amtex CM were not invited to rebuild a new plant in the city.

Tapor and Krasow

To the world's surprise, the small nation of Tapor was more than holding its own against the large neighbouring invader.

Its small, well-trained and well-armed army out-fought and out-thought from its assumed inferior position. Its effective defensive capability was actually depleting the size of the invading force. Strategically, it intended to do this until the enemy was sufficiently weakened for it to go on the offensive. The high command of the aggressor knew this and planned an action to make it impossible. At 7:30 a.m. on a Tuesday morning, it launched six cruise missiles against the small nation's only nuclear power station to turn it into a 'dirty bomb'. As a result of the radiation released, mass destruction of the population was expected.

Arguments have raged for years on the risk posed by nuclear power plants. One camp argues they are completely safe and would remain so even if attacked – the heavily reinforced concrete shell of their reactor being claimed as bomb-proof. The other camp presents evidence that contradicts this assertion. The reality is that if power is cut and the cooling system fails, spent fuel rods would overheat, resulting in a meltdown of the reactor. This would then release radioactive gases and aerosols into the atmosphere. It is this latter view that provided the 'rationale' for the invader's intent to strike. The moment to do this centred on wind direction delivering the maximum exposure to the maximum number of the enemy's civilian population. The strike was made at 7:55 on a Monday morning in August. But at 8:10 a.m. the wind changed direction. Two border villages were seriously affected. There was no major impact on the population of Tapor and Tapor City, but a huge one on the aggressor's forces massed in the border city of Krasow. Ten thousand troops ended up dying. The long-term health of large numbers of its population was also seriously compromised for many years to come. Effectively, a small city lost the bulk of its population. Likewise, many animals died, and the entire food system around it was effectively contaminated. The event did not end the war, but it did settle the debate on the risk of nuclear power stations in conflict zones.

Industrial Environments

RANGERVILLE

The city lived by, and on top of an iron ore mine. The mining activity was almost directly below the city and extended to a depth of 380 metres. The city was built during the same period in which the mine was constructed. Ore from the mine has been extracted continuously for a century and a half. During this time, the mine had constantly grown. Its growth mirrored the growth of the city. What went unrecognised was that the city was being constructed directly above the mine. Unsurprisingly, the weight of the city added to the mass above the mine. For many decades, there was no awareness that the geological structure below the city was unstable. One hundred and sixty-two years and thirty-one days after the mine opened, this structural problem dramatically announced itself. Inevitably, this day of crisis was destined to arrive.

. . .

Elisa had just dropped her daughter Kelly off at her school and was driving into the city to the clinic where she worked as a speech therapist. It was a fifteen-minute drive; she was just over halfway and had stopped in a line of cars waiting at a red light. There was a very loud, deep rumbling sound getting ever louder, and the ground was shaking. Suddenly, instead of maybe ten or twelve cars in front of her, there was no red light and only four. She hesitated for maybe five seconds, opened the car door and ran. People in the car behind her were doing the same. Further back, some drivers were trying to reverse and crashed into cars behind them. There were screams, yelling, sirens and the relentless sound of a city collapsing and falling into an expanding sinkhole. People were running in all directions. Somebody knocked over an old lady in a wheelchair. Elisa stopped, picked her up, put her in the chair, telling her to hang on, and ran, pushing the lady before her.

Megan, the old lady, had badly grazed her hands and face when she fell on the road. She was bleeding, the right side of her face was swelling and her eye was closing. Elisa stopped outside the post office, which was at least a kilometre from the hole, and phoned 333, the emergency service number to call for an ambulance. She was told, after being asked if the person's condition was life-threatening, and answering in the negative, that a code red disaster was now in force and she could expect a wait of up to two hours. Elisa stayed with Megan until the ambulance came at 11:50. During this time, she asked for help from a post office worker, who brought a bottle of water and a first aid kit. Elisa washed Megan's hands, bandaged them and bathed her cheek and eye, which now was even more swollen and was totally closed. Megan was dazed, but before the paramedics placed her in the ambulance, she emotionally and profusely thanked Elisa.

It took Elisa an hour and a half to walk home. Thankfully, her cell phone worked. *En route*, she called Kelly's school. The line was engaged; on the fifth try, by which time she was home, she got through. There was just a recorded message: 'All children as are safe. If you are in a position to collect your child please do so as soon as possible. The school will care for all children not collected, and contact the police and social services.' The school was a twenty-minute walk away; Elisa set off immediately.

On returning home with Kelly, who wanted answers to questions she did not have, she made a pot of tea and turned the TV on. Nothing, no power. At least the phone network was okay. There was a small battery-powered radio in the bathroom. All stations were presenting continuous coverage of the disaster event. They reported that over 20 per cent of the central business district had fallen into the sinkhole, and 800 people, and still counting, had died, with over 1,500 having been injured escaping from damaged buildings or in traffic accidents. Ground movement had produced cracks in many buildings and roads within a radius of 700 to 800 metres from the hole. The situation around it remained unstable; every now and again, another chunk of the city fell into it. Mostly a small piece of road or building, but occasionally there was a large chunk. An exclusion zone 1500 metres back from the hole had been created. Power, water and gas had all been cut off, this for an indefinite period. Over 10,000 people living close to the hole were evacuated to temporary emergency shelters.

Two days after the event, the entire central area of the city was designated as unsafe and to be permanently abandoned. The result was that nine suburban areas lacked an urban centre where they could buy food. They had a phone network, but no other services or public transport.

Elisa, a single mother, now had no job. Her clinic was in the exclusion zone. She had no car and a house without more than a few days' food. She phoned her sister, Kate, once she returned home with Kelly. Kate lived with Danny, her husband and their twins, Shana and Grace, in a house on the market garden in Mardon, a village 33 kilometres west of the city. Danny had inherited the business from his father. He arrived two hours after the call and picked up Elisa and Kelly. They were to live with the family for the next four months.

Rather than sell the produce, Danny and Kate grew it and then added value. They made jams, pickled vegetables, bottled fruit, dried herbs, as well as having a stall at the local weekly farmers' market. They supplied twelve health food stores with their products.

The business was doing well, enough for Kate to give up her job as a dental nurse.

Two years after the disaster, not much had changed, except for the arrival of another kind of disaster – this one a financial one. Thousands of people in Rangerville had lost their jobs, and many also lost members of their families and their homes. Those living in risk areas owned properties that were now of little value and unsellable, while still having mortgages to repay. Many banks repossessed houses that were unable to be sold. Most leased them to their former owners at a peppercorn rent. One thousand and twenty-seven people had died immediately during the disaster or later from injuries. The centre of the city was now being followed by the slow death of the remainder. The expectation is that eventually everything will disappear into the hole. People in a position to move away did so. A retail centre was created in a box building on an industrial estate, a government assistance programme was established and a five-year demolition and reconstruction programme was announced

Elisa and Kelly returned home once services were restored. Her car insurance company honoured her claim, and she found another job at a health centre nearer her home. None of the parents at Kelly's school had lost their lives during the disaster.

SONELLA

The City of Sonella had a one-dimensional economy: coal. The deep mine had dominated the city for numerous decades. Located three miles from the centre of the city was three miles from the mine, its economy depended upon it and had done so for decades. When the mine closed, within weeks, did a third at least 20 per cent of the local businesses did so as well. This list of closures included three pubs, a local laundry, a sports club, a gym, a betting shop, two cafes, two trucking companies and three small engineering businesses.

Walk down any street in the centre of the city and you could immediately see the city was having a hard time. You just had to read the graffiti on boarded-up shop window, which was everywhere. The streets were dirty, homelessness was visible and the smell of poverty was in the air. People looked and felt depressed. It was obvious the local Council was broke and broken.

When the mine closed without notice, the company laid off the entire workforce without any severance pay, closed the gates and walked away. The mine was not properly decommissioned. Over time, gas started to build up. Then there were noises. The mine flooded and started to collapse, and sound was being transmitted above ground. The Council sought advice from a mining engineering company, and they suggested it should be assessed robotically. The robots used sensors and video capability. The data and images would give a good indication of the state of the mine and the level of risk. The fear was that a major collapse in the mine would result in subsidence that would affect the city. The Council accepted the suggestion from the company and commissioned them to undertake the inspection by a robot.

The robot had been in the mine for one hour and eight minutes when the explosion happened at 8:52 a.m. The inquiry that took place fourteen months after the event stated in a 400-page report that it could not have come from the solid-state electronics of the robot, but that the machine may have done something that caused a spark. However, the cause of ignition was recorded as unknown. The explosion collapsed the entire mine. This effectively caused a mini-earthquake, and numerous buildings collapsed. Twenty-seven people died, fourteen of them children, fifty-seven adults and eleven children were injured. The children were in the school playground waiting for the first class of the day to start. Water mains burst, power was cut. This event sounded the death knell for the already struggling city. It froze, and the city froze; everything stopped.

The state government convened an emergency cabinet meeting. It met on the evening of the disaster and announced that a commission of inquiry would immediately commence. It also announced it would send a team of grief counsellors to the city, with a specialist group assigned to the school. It instructed the National Institute for Scientific and Technical Research to send an assessment team, and likewise one from the State Department of Mineral Resources. The federal government informed the state government that it had ordered the Federal Police to commence an investigation, with specific reference to the conduct of the mining company. Finally, it announced all flags to be flown at half-mast in the nation for one week, and that it would provide additional funding to assist with the recovery process. All of this activity was important, but little consolation to the families and friends who had lost loved ones. The immediate concern of the City Council at the time of the disaster was with the surviving children. Seven parents were among the dead. The entire city was in shock.

The city never recovered. Workers left looking for employment elsewhere, as did young families and young people. Businesses continued to close. Within two years, the population of the city was a mix of old people, the infirm and the unemployable. The retail sector had shrunk to one supermarket, a dozen shops and one pub. The hospital was only partly functioning, and the police force was a third of its original size. An administrator had taken over from a dysfunctional city Council. The city was just waiting for the old people to die and was disappearing in slow motion.

Technology and Disappearance

SPHERE BETA

For people like me living in Sphere Beta, it's hard to remember what learning used to be like. With neuro-connect and embedded AI with memory function, schools are a thing of the past. What your knowledge quotient is deemed to be is predicated upon an assessment of tested brain reception capacity and patterned capability. Regulated knowledge input is assigned to a lifelong learning programme. Knowledge is no longer a requirement of functional life within the Sphere environment. It arrives as a driver and mechanism of selected preoccupations (a hyper-sophisticated form of what once were called hobbies) that 'make life meaningful' and as such constitute a surrogate for 'labour'.

Broadcast education, socialisation and communication training, and creative workshop immersion are the pedagogic orders of the day. Well, at least for the young people of the Sphere Beta city system. The days of the pluriverse, the notion of the coexistence of multiple worlds, are over. There was never a condition of compatible difference. Now in the age of the triadic fracture zones, not even the fiction survives. My world has retracted into the techno-sphere of environmental protection, inhabited by corporate elites and their service providers. This is a world where billions of people, mostly from the global south, have been abandoned. They survive by any means possible; many don't. They have camps and are nomadic. Then there are the masses who struggle to survive by adaptive means in old cities. Some do well; others do not.

Once 'smart cities' were about traffic management and risk reduction; now they have become totally integrated systems management for power, waste, health, policing, defence and industrial production.

The world outside the bubble of the sphere is a hostile zone for us, only knowable by eye-sky monitoring and TEATA (threat evaluative assessment technology and action). The Sphere Beta is a total defence environment providing protection from the hostile enviroclimatic and socio-biological environment external to it. At the same time, internal domain urban and domestic sensors, linked to neuro-connectors, identify and respond to body-biofunction and psycho-emotional needs. Data gathered directs diet and food delivery; exercise machine settings; medication requirements; and chemoemotional regulation. Everyone is kept fit, healthy and emotionally stable and secure.

The organic and the artificial, the biological and the technical; the domestic and the urban; the individual and the collective; the physical and the mental – none of these binary relations exist any longer in the post-transhuman life of the sphere and its bio-transcendent techno-species. Beings no longer just work, play and occupy the city, for it also occupies them. Life for the 'people' of the sphere has become a total networked condition of being. Wherever you are, everything is present. You are in the city, and it is inside you.

So, what's the point of learning in this all-providing environment? Machines do everything. But they cannot create things of meaningless meaning to anyone other than their creator. Yes, they can simulate art, poetry, literature and music, but they can't create what they symbolically and emotionally mean to people. The domain of learning here becomes one of resistance to individuation by 'the culture machine'. So cast this learning as undirected imagination, emotional investment, unproductive labour as pleasure, and of all those activities of making to maintain sanity in a mechanised world of function without sense.

ALPHA CITY 12

This city is one of the first total AI-created cities, of which at present there are 487. There is little to say about it. In reality, the city is a robot-serviced retirement home for young, middle-aged and old people who have been deemed as the 'useless class'. These are people whose jobs have been totally replaced by machines and who are classified as having no functional value. All their needs are met in what is an environment of entertainment. After assignment, and on arrival, a block and apartment is allocated (single or family), and a health and behaviour monitoring correction chip is injected (to counter aggression and depression). A bitcoin allowance is given (based on the value of an individual's liquidated assets).

The city has everything: from pool to golf, tennis and swimming, to go-karting, indoor climbing and archery, to wood carving, pottery, painting, embroidery, dressmaking, cookery and clubs. There are theatres, movies, dance and concert halls, ice rinks and roller skating, a bowls club, book clubs and debating societies, plus chess, darts, Go, bridge, poker and scrabble clubs. There are 3D acting classes, writing programmes, modern dance, yoga and Tai Chi. There are bars, cafes, coffee shops, ice cream parlours, four 'restrictive needs' shopping malls, and so much more.

The amenities include four parks and gardens, six sports clubs and grounds, three golf courses, eight gyms, four indoor and outdoor swimming pools, four hospitals and a crematorium.

Nobody could ever imagine a desert to be so populated with so many 'riches', yet be unmarked by history and the touch of the hand.

NOTES

Preface

1. Italo Calvino, *Invisible Cities*, trans. William Weaver (London: Vintage Books, 1997; originally published 1972).

2. Thomas Kyd, *The Spanish Tragedy*, 1587, https://www.gutenberg.org/files /6043/6043-h/6043-h.htm released 2009.

3. Cambridge Centre for Risk Studies, *World Cities at Risk, 2015–2025* (Cambridge: University of Cambridge Judge Business School, 2015).

4. Savills, *Resilient Cities Index 2021*, http://www.savills.com/impacts/market -trends/resilience-ranked.html (accessed January 11, 2025).

5. The new capital, Nusantara, is currently under construction.

6. The relation between fact/non-fiction and the fictive/fiction is especially problematic in addressing climate change, as Amitav Ghosh argued in *The Great Derangement* (Chicago: The University of Chicago Press, 2016).

7. 'All that is solid melts into Air' is a famous line from Karl Marx and Friedrich Engels, "Manifesto of the Communist Party," in *Marx/Engels Selected Works*, vol. 1, trans. Samuel Moore in cooperation with Frederick Engels (Moscow: Progress Publishers, 1969), 16. Originally published in 1848.

8. Kant's theory of the imagination has influenced numerous philosophers over the past two and a half centuries. Kant conceived as a pervasive mental that spanned and functioned across many of the cognitive and empirical aspects of our lives. As such, it figured in his address to pure and practical reason. Immanuel Kant, *Critique of Pure Reason* (The Cambridge Edition of the Works of Immanuel Kant), trans. and ed. Paul Guyer and Allen W. Wood (Cambridge: Cambridge University Press, 1999; originally published 1781); Immanuel Kant, *Critique of Practical Reason*, trans. Mary J. Gregor (Cambridge: Cambridge University Press, 2015; originally published 1788).

FURTHER READING: AN ANNOTATED LIST

Danowski, Déborah and Eduardo Viveiros De Castro (2017), *The Ends of the World*, Oxford: Polity (an inter-cultural engagement with climate, crisis and 'us').

Erickson, Chris (2002), *The Poetics of Fear*, New York: Continuum (fear of the future, not least from climate chaos, is widespread—this book is about resisting it).

Fry, Tony (2015), *City Future in the Age of a Changing Climate*, London: Routledge (cities are going to dramatically change, this book makes this clear).

Fry, Tony (2017), *Remaking Cities*, London: Bloomsbury (this book introduces 'metrofitting,' a method of remaking cities).

Fry, Tony (2022), *Writing Design Fiction, Relocating a City in Crisis*, London: Bloomsbury (design fiction here is shown as a means to understand complexity and directional change).

Fry, Tony (2025), *Political Breakout, Situation Need, Action*, Wilmington (DE): Vernon Press.

Ghosh, Amitav (2016), *The Great Derangement*, Chicago: Chicago University Press (an interesting discussion on climate change, the unthinkable and fiction).

Read, Stephen and Camilo Pinilla (eds) (2006), *Visualising Urban Space*, Amsterdam: TechnePress (how cities are seen now is no guide to how they will be visualised in the future).

Robinson, Kim Stanley (2020), *The Ministry For The Future*, London: Little Brown Book Group (this book is an example of hybrid fact/fiction fusion that help the future to be imagined).

Shirreff, General Sir Richard (2016), *War with Russia*, London: Hodder and Stoughton (this book is another example of hybrid fact/fiction fusion that help the future to be imagined).

Steele, Wendy, John Handmer and Ian McShane (2023), *Hot Cities*, Cheltenham: Edward Elgar (the problem of cities getting hotter cannot be 'solved' by the same methods that created them).